BALLERINA, BALLERINA

Marko Sosič

Translated by Maja Visenjak Limon

DALKEY ARCHIVE PRESS
Champaign / London / Dublin

Originally published in Slovenian as *Balerina, Balerina* by Mladika, Trieste, 1997

Copyright © 1997 by Mladika, Trieste

Translation copyright © 2014 by Maja Visenjak Limon

First edition, 2014

Library of Congress Cataloging-in-Publication Data

Sosič, Marko, 1958-
    [Balerina, balerina. English]
    Ballerina, ballerina / by Marko Sosič ; translated by Maja Visenjak Limon. -- First edition.
    pages cm
    "Originally published in Slovenian as Balerina, Balerina by Mladika, Trieste, 1997"
    --Title page verso.
    ISBN 978-1-62897-097-5 (pbk. : alk. paper)
    I. Visenjak-Limon, Maja, translator. II. Title.
    PG1919.29.A5B3513 2014
    891.8'415--dc23

                          2014014008

Partially funded by the Illinois Arts Council, a state agency, and by the University of Illinois at Urbana-Champaign

In cooperation with the Slovene Writers' Association – Litteræ Slovenicæ Series

This work has been published with the support of the Trubar Foundation, located at the Slovene Writers' Association, Ljubljana, Slovenia.

Ta knjiga je bila objavljena s pomočjo Trubarjevega sklada pri Društvu slovenskih pisateljev, Ljubljana, Slovenija.

This translation has been financially supported by JAK the Slovenian Book Agency

J A K

www.dalkeyarchive.com

Cover: design and composition by Mikhail Iliatov
Printed on permanent/durable acid-free paper

BALLERINA, BALLERINA

AAAAH! I'M FALLING. I grab at clouds, raindrops, hailstones, sunbeams, I keep waving my arms. It doesn't help. I'm falliiing. Below me is a field, it's getting closer and closer, the horse chestnut tree in the yard, the house, the path leading from the village past the church straight into the yard and to the house. I see the roof with big stones on it because of the wind. No more clouds, raindrops, no more sunshine. I have nothing to hold on to. I wave my arms, faster and faster. It doesn't help. I see the moon. It's shining. Shining on the roof and on the tree top that is getting closer. I'll fall into the tree and wake the birds. Ohhhh. Through the roof. I'll break through the roof. Now. I suddenly wake up. I'm lying by the bed. I fell off the bed, like before, like now. I'm not scared, I just have to go and pee.

I open my eyes and look at the ceiling. I can't see any hole I might have made. I look at the window. It looks the same as always. It's morning. I see the top of the chestnut tree. The birds have not flown away. They're only just waking up. I'm not afraid, I just have to go and pee, like always when a new day starts. I close my eyes. I'm glad the window is still there, that outside is the tree top with the birds and that I have not broken through the roof. I know. I feel warm. Maybe it's spring in the yard, maybe summer. It's not winter. When it's winter, it's cold and the chestnut tree in the yard has no leaves and Mama puts stockings on my legs. It's warm. Suddenly. I wet myself on the floor by the bed I have fallen from. I hear footsteps, Ivanka is coming from the kitchen, up the stone stairs, and she stops at the door, opening it slightly. She looks at me, I know. Mama. Ivanka is my mama. I recognize her because I've wet myself, and because that's what I have done, it must be a new day. And if it really is all true, Mama always opens the door slightly and looks into my room.

I watch her walking toward me. Behind her, everything is blue. From the morning. The wooden closet with a mirror, the closet with drawers, the chair. Everything is blue. Mama is blue, too. The hair that she's combed in the kitchen and pushed into a bun, her eyes, her mouth, her hands. Her hands are also colored blue by the morning.

She lifts me. She holds me under my arms, lifting me. I laugh. Mama laughs, too. She can't lift me because she's laughing. Then she says: Help me, and laughs even harder. We're sitting on the floor by the bed, laughing. I look at her. I see tears in her eyes. They're full of light. I touch them. I touch her eyes and the tears and the light, and I hear, not right now while she's laughing. I hear her talking to someone next to the kitchen door. I'm standing in the corner, then. I'm standing on tiptoe, looking at the kitchen door. Mama is talking. I don't know who's with her. I can't see her face. I'm standing on tiptoe, looking at the bun on her head, her shoulders, her skirt and her slippers. They say that's how it is, says Mama. They say it happens sometimes. All of a sudden and no one really knows why. Out of the blue. She doesn't play anymore. She keeps herself to herself, who knows what she's thinking. You ask her and she doesn't say. She hears everything, but she doesn't talk anymore. She laughs, she cries, but you don't know when or why. You don't know what she's thinking, what's going through her head … They say it'll get worse every year, says Mama, more quietly, and I stand up even higher on my tiptoes to see her face. I hear Mama's last words. Look at her! She spends hours and hours standing on tiptoe, does everything I tell her to, then she goes in that corner, lifts herself onto her toes and just stays there. There's nothing they can do, they say … that sometimes it just happens with children. At that moment Mama turns to me. I'm standing on my tiptoes and I can see her face. There are tears in her eyes then, too, and her smile, and I hear Mama's words. What will happen to us, Ballerina, eh?

I no longer hear her words now. Just our laughter, and I see the tears in her eyes. They're full of light.

Mama stands up, using her arms and legs. Come on, Ballerina, she says: It's your party today!

She leads me down the stairs, to the washbasin in the hall. Then she undresses and washes me, talking to me. She says I'm fifteen years old, that it's April, that I was born in the middle of spring and that I have to look pretty today. She dresses me in a pink dress with a bow at the side. Oh, how beautiful our Ballerina looks, she says as she combs my hair. I'm looking in the mirror that hangs on a nail on the wall. I think I look like Mama. She's combing my hair, talking. Mama says I will be beautiful today because it's my party and it's spring on the other side of the door that is still closed, in the yard and in the field. She says it has been dug, the field, and it smells nice because it has rested and no longer has any weeds. She keeps combing my hair. I'm looking in the mirror. I see the field, blue from the morning, the weeds, tall and thin; every time my mother pulls the comb through my hair there are fewer weeds and I know it's going to be a new day. And I see the dug field in front of me, I see it in one part of the mirror, where my face is and Mama's face, which presses itself against mine, talking, the face that is Mama's. We'll put on a bit of perfume, she says, touching my neck with her fingers. It's Mennen, says Mama, *dopobarba*, aftershave, but it smells like perfume. Mmmmm, says Mama, after, you smell so nice, our Ballerina. And I no longer see her, Mama, in the mirror that hangs on a nail on the wall, I know she's walking into the kitchen, telling me to come, saying I'm beautiful, telling me to sit at the table, she'll give me coffee and then, she says, we'll have visitors in the afternoon and I'll get presents and Ivan will come.

I think Ivan is here already. I look toward the kitchen. We're standing by the door, then, I don't know when, because I don't know how many new days have passed since and how many times I wet myself because it was morning. I know we're standing by the door and Ivan says we must measure ourselves to see who is tallest. Ivan is small. He's a child, I think, something could happen to him. I must protect him. And I stand on tiptoe and everyone says: Oh, our Ballerina is growing so quickly! Ivan is laughing and says he'll be a doctor and will cure me when he grows up, and everyone claps.

I look in the mirror. Once more. My hair is combed. I look toward the kitchen. I step through the door and into the corner by the stove. That's the best place.

I look at the door from there, standing on my tiptoes. Then it hurts. I grab whatever I can find and throw it at the door. I nearly always hit the door. If it's a plate, it breaks. Mama picks it up and strokes the door. She's always saying it needs painting. The door and the kitchen, everything. It needs painting white, she says.

I'm in the corner now, where it's nice. My toes aren't hurting. It's just Mama in the kitchen. I know what she's doing. She's washing handkerchiefs in boiling water because *Tata*, my father, coughs and spits into them. He also spits outside the door, sometimes. He's not here now. He's in the bar, with friends. Playing cards, says Mama. He'll come for lunch, like always when it's a new day. Mama says he'll choke with coughing. I see him, coughing in the hall, always, then he comes to the kitchen and looks through the window. He doesn't speak, just says to me: How are you, my Ballerina? And he looks out of the window. I know Mama will hang the handkerchiefs on a line in the yard, later.

The postman comes first. Nearly always when it's a new day. The postman talks, drinks and then goes through the door. Then Mama hangs the handkerchiefs in the yard and I look through the kitchen window, from my corner. I see the handkerchiefs and think that *Tata* is home. In bits on the handkerchiefs ... After the postman is gone.

The postman is here now. I can hear his footsteps. I'm afraid of the postman because he has a cap and heavy shoes. Mama is already getting a glass ready. He'll come in, talking and then he'll drink. Then he won't be able to breathe, after drinking, and he'll laugh and say: O la la!

He's here. Hello, Ivanka, he says and puts something on the table. Mama says she doesn't believe the advertisement and that her name would never be chosen and she would never get the millions. Mama is pouring the drink. *Schnapps*, she says. The postman is looking into the glass, talking.

I stand on tiptoe. I listen.

So? How's our Ballerina doing? He looks at me. I don't want him to look at me. Then he looks at Mama. She's still stirring the handkerchiefs in the boiling water. I see her. Ivanka, have you heard the latest? They say man is going to the moon, but it won't be anytime soon.

Oh yeah? says Mama, staring at the boiling water. I see her.

Yes. Not for another year or so, I don't know when. But tell me, why does anyone have to go to the moon?

Well, I don't know. Maybe there's too many of us ...

On earth?

I don't know. Maybe.

Mama continues stirring. With a wooden spoon. I see her. I see her nose, chin, forehead, arm. The postman shifts, takes his glass and downs it. Everything in the glass. I watch him. He can't breathe, he opens his mouth and holds it open, for a long time. He breathes in and then out. Then he smiles, Hey there, he says. He gets up, adjusts his cap. He says something else. To me. I think he says it to me because he's looking at me. I don't want him to look at me, I don't want him to say something to me. I stand on tiptoe, even higher. High. I'm shaking. I can't stand on tiptoe for that long.

Hey there, our little Ballerina, eh? What are you going to say, eh? And he laughs. My toes are hurting. He goes on. What do you say, shall we go? Shall we go to the moon? Would you go to the moon, eh? Oh, you would, you would go. Well, if we have to, we'll go, did you hear what your mother said? That there are too many of us! And if there are so many of us, there won't be enough to eat and we'll have to go to the Mooon.

I watch him. Bye, Ivanka, he says and goes out the door. Then. I can no longer stand on tiptoe. I grab a glass on the table. I throw it at the door. The glass breaks.

Oh, Ballerina, Ballerina, says Mama, sweeping up the bits of the glass.

I watch her. I'm afraid that if there isn't enough to eat we'll have to go to the moon. Not for another year or so, said the postman. I don't know what a year is. Not one year, not another year … I don't know.

Mama throws the bits of glass in the garbage. She looks at me. She comes closer, adjusts my hair, strokes me. I feel her hand on my cheek. Oh, my Ballerina, you mustn't be afraid, we won't go to the moon, we'll stay here as long as God lets us. Me and you and all of us.

Mama knows what I think. Sometimes. She knows. So do I. I know she wants me to laugh, not cry. But I can't laugh because the postman knows everything and because he said what he said. Mama moves. I watch her. She takes the handkerchiefs out of the boiling water and goes through the door. Now I'm not afraid anymore. The handkerchiefs are already hanging one next to the other. My *Tata*.

I look through the window. I can't see Mama. Suddenly. All I see are the handkerchiefs. I look around the kitchen. I touch the bow on my pink dress. I look. I see the stove, the table, the refrigerator and the ashtray on it, the cupboard with plates and glasses. Spoons are there, too. I see a small shelf. On the shelf is a box from which talking and singing comes. But only when *Tata* presses a button. Turn on the Grundig, he says to Mama, let's hear the weather forecast. On the box, there is a boat. Mama calls it a gondola. She says they have such boats in Venice, but they don't have the lights, the boats in Venice. Our gondola has lights and sometimes they shine. I look at the slightly open door. Mama is here again. She says lunch will be soon, *Tata* will come, Karlo will come from work, Srečko will come with his mama, Josipina will come, and Aunt Elizabeta and then, when there's cake, Ivan will also come. Here's *Tata*. I can hear him. He's coughing and spitting. He says he's old and sits down. He says I should sit next to him, like always when it is a new day. And I do, always. Now he says I'm beautiful, I'm a big girl, and he holds my hand. Then he coughs again in the hall and returns to the kitchen with tears from the coughing and takes my hand again. What's new, Ballerina, he says. And I take hold of his ear. I like squeezing his ear. He bends over to me, smiling, when he isn't coughing. And I squeeze his ear. *Basta, basta*, enough, Ballerina, he says when it hurts and I twist his ear even more because I like it and I'm calm when I'm twisting his ear, I know.

Mama is setting the table. She says I should put the glasses and plates out. Now she knows I won't throw them at the door, she knows now that I'll put them on the table. I take a plate. Each one separately. Mama says, put it here. I do. The same with every plate.

Always when it is a new day, I put plates on the table. Today, now, too. It seems to me that I hear my voice as I'm putting down the plates. As if I have said something. My ears ring when I have this feeling. Now, too. I'm wearing a pink dress, I have a bow at the side and I'm putting a plate on the table and my ears are ringing. I have to sing, then they won't ring anymore. That's what I must do. They also sing in the box with the gondola on top. Not always. First, Tata says turn on the Grundig, and then they sing *Vooolare, ooooho, can-*

tare, o,o,o,o, nel blu dipinto di blu, felice di stare lassù … I hear, always when the Grundig is turned on, I hear them sing, and Mama says it's always the same song on the radio.

I leave the plate on the table. I step into the corner, on tiptoe, and I sing. Loud. I shout, *VOOOlaree, o, o!!!* Like the Grundig. Then my ears don't ring anymore. Inside my ears. Mama lets me sing. She knows it won't be for long. When it's lunch, I only sing twice.

Karlo comes. Through the door. I see him. Mama says he's my brother. He comes from the woods, Karlo does, I know. Mama says he guards the woods. He looks at me like he always does when it's a new day. Karlo. I don't want him to look at me. I run into him. Now. And I push him through the door into the yard. He comes back, strokes me. It's OK, it's OK, Ballerina, he says. Sometimes he stays in the yard. I see him through the window, spooning the *minestra* into his mouth. He sits on the bench under the chestnut tree, slurping the *minestra*, and then he returns to the woods, because he has to guard them. Mama says that Karlo is older, that he's forty years old, that I'm the youngest, that my sister Josipina is also older, Mama says. Albert is also my brother. Mama says he's the oldest. He won't come to lunch because he's in Australia, Mama says.

I don't know who Albert is, I don't know what Australia is.

Karlo and *Tata* are here. They're sitting at the table. Mama says we should wait for the others. Elizabeta comes. Mama says that she and Elizabeta are sisters. Ivanka and Elizabeta. Mama says that it's not quite sixty years since they were born. I don't know what that means. Mama says she wants to go to Ajdovščina once more, where she and Elizabeta were born, because it's not far. Karlo has a car, he could take her, and Elizabeta, Mama says in the evening as we stand by the window in the room. I will go, too, Mama says, but first I have to have my photograph taken for a border pass, she says. Karlo sometimes takes me to Elizabeta, I know. I know Elizabeta. She's like Mama. Karlo takes me to Elizabeta in the car. Mama says the car is not Karlo's. But it isn't far. Mama says that everyone is close by, that there aren't many of us and that we're all close by.

Elizabeta kisses me and puts a bag next to the door. In the bag is something for me because it's my party, I know. Elizabeta then sits at the table. I don't know which is my mama. Suddenly.

I hear footsteps. Laughter. I recognize it. Srečko. Mama says he's already drunk. He's coming through the door. He doesn't say anything. He just laughs and comes into the kitchen. His mother, Aunt Lucija, is with him. Mama says that Aunt Lucija is my father's sister and therefore she's my aunt and Srečko is my cousin. Srečko is laughing and looking at me. Lucija says to him: Sit down, sit at the table. I watch Aunt Lucija. She's wearing slippers like mine. With a butterfly. Mama says she's forgotten to put her shoes on again, the poor thing …

In the evening, when Mama and I are looking through the window and she's talking to me quietly, because, she says, Karlo is asleep, *Tata* is asleep and even the birds in the chestnut tree are asleep, she says she doesn't know what will happen to Srečko when Aunt Lucija is gone. Mama says Aunt Lucija will die because she's old and forgets to put her shoes on.

Now I'm watching Aunt Lucija, she's pushing Srečko toward the table and says to me, because she's looking at me: Oh, Ballerina, how beautiful you are today, and she sits next to Srečko. He keeps laughing, but a little more quietly now. Karlo is also laughing quietly and so is *Tata*. Everyone laughs when Srečko is here.

Ivanka, do you know where I found him? says Lucija.

No, says Ivanka, my mother.

In the square!

Surely not?!

Yes … he was there, in the middle of the square, looking toward the sea, trembling. Like a leaf.

Is he still afraid?

Yes, still … I tell him to go and buy some bread and he gets lost and then I don't know where he is. I have to get dressed and put my shoes on and go looking for him.

Srečko is still laughing, still quietly. I'm standing in the corner, looking at him and listening.

If the road is too wide or if it's a square, he's afraid. He can't go on. Everything that is wide and big. I tell him, stay home, but he goes and gets lost and then stands there trembling, calling me … You know, what happened in Spain. He said he was going to Spain. He took the train, got to Spain and just stopped at the station. One day. A whole day. As he reached the station exit, he saw a square and didn't dare go out. He was scared, I know. If it's a square, he's scared. And then he took the train back. From station to station. Seventeen hours on the train. Now you tell me that he isn't crazy!

Everyone is laughing now. Srečko very loudly.

And then he has to have a drink, says Lucija, and he's drunk. Oh, Ballerina, Ballerina, what would you say, eh?

And I look at her slippers with a butterfly, like mine.

I tell him, says Lucija, listen to music. If you can't work, if I can't even send you for a loaf of bread, listen to music. What can you do, he likes it. Silvester was just like him. The organ and nothing else. In church all day long … On the organ. And this one is just like him, just like Silvester. May he rest in peace, he did leave me a pension.

I look at the window. I hear footsteps. I know it's Josipina. She always runs, my sister does.

In the evening, when Mama and I are looking through the window in the room where I sleep, and Mama is talking to me quietly, she says that Josipina secretly does the ironing for the watchmaker's wife. She says Josipina's husband doesn't want her to do the ironing for other people and wants her to be at home, but she still goes, secretly. Mama says her husband is big and strong. I don't know who he is. He's not in the kitchen today. He never is. Only Josipina runs here sometimes. She has something to eat, then she runs back. I've only got two more things to do, says Josipina and then runs. She irons two things and runs home. In the evening by the window above the chestnut tree, Mama says that Josipina's husband was on a ship when there was a war, that he shot at planes and that he gets nervous at night, because he still sees them up in the sky and shoots at them from his bed. Mama says that he's Italian because he's called Giacomino.

Now she's here, in the kitchen. Josipina. Breathing. Deeply. She laughs. She comes to me. Happy Birthday, Ballerina, she says and gives me a bunch of flowers. She says they're tulips. Oh, how beautiful they are, says Elizabeta and puts her hands on her knees. I got a letter, says Josipina, breathing. From Albert. From Australia, she says. What does he say? asks Karlo. I watch her. Her eyes are shining. He says he's coming in a year or so. For a visit. And she sits down. No one talks. In the evening, when we stand by the window, Mama says that Albert also used to guard the woods, like Karlo. Then, says Mama, he went to Australia, with a *signorina* from Istria. And then she cries, does Mama. Then she says that Karlo started guarding the woods and he got Albert's job. Because there was no one else to do it.

Now everyone is here, says Mama in the kitchen. And she brings a pan to the table. *Tata* is looking out of the window, I see him.

Is *signorina* coming with him? he asks.

He didn't write anything about her, says Josipina.

And then everyone is quiet. We're sitting at the table. Srečko is quietly laughing, then everyone laughs and eats, everyone. And we laugh.

Then we don't laugh anymore. Just eat. Soup. I squeeze my spoon with my whole hand, bringing the soup to my mouth and slurping it off. *Tata* says I should eat slowly. I'd like to stand on tiptoe, there in the corner. And sing. I don't sing. I want to hold his ear. I hold his ear. I'm thinking of the postman, of the moon, I think about how there will be no more room on earth and we won't have anything to eat. I slurp the soup. Faster. Still holding the ear of the man who is my *tata*.

Later, there'll be cake. After lunch. Ivan will come then. Mama says he's in school now. She says I used to be there, too. Not now. Later. They said I'd go to school again, but I have to grow first. They said when I'm big, I'll go to school, Mama says. In the evening when we're looking through the window, she says there's still time. When it's a new day, says Mama, that's when I'll go to school.

Tata takes my hand and puts it on the table. I can see him feeling his ear. It hurts. I look at Elizabeta. I see Mama. I don't know which is Mama and which Elizabeta. She also has her hair in a bun. I look at her hands. She says they're rough. I know what it's like at Elizabeta's, when Karlo takes me to her when Mama is tired, when she says she loves me, but she needs a rest. Karlo also says Mama has to rest, that she can't wash me every day, pick up bits of plates from the floor in front of the door and sing. Mama sings with me and I'm not scared any more, I know. We stand in the hall and sing. Both of us. We hold hands and sing. Loudly. In the hall. Me and Mama. Then Mama is tired and Karlo takes me to Elizabeta's in the car.

In the evening, when Mama and I stand by the window, she tells me that she and Elizabeta came to Trieste together. From Ajdovščina. To Trieste. When they were really young girls. Mama says that she and Elizabeta cleaned other people's houses. They washed, cooked and ironed, like Josipina. But not secretly. Then Mama used to go and get milk from the house in which we are now, she says. Milk for the lady she ironed for, and once she was told that she should come again, for milk, that Franc would come, that he was handsome and that they would marry. Then, Mama says, Franc came from the army and he was handsome and they did marry. Franc is my *Tata*, the one whose ear I pull. Mama says that he plays cards in the village, in the bar. That he even goes to play in Venice. Not now, because he's old, Mama says. Mama says that *Tata* brought the gondola with the lights which now stands on the Grundig in the kitchen. Franc. Once upon a time.

Then I stop looking at Elizabeta. I don't want to go to Elizabeta's. I don't want Mama to be tired and Karlo to take me to Elizabeta's.

I sit, crumbling bread. I eat the crumbs, slowly. I roll them around my mouth and then swallow them, the crumbs. I watch Srečko. He's talking. He says that Beethoven is the greatest composer. Now he's crying. Aunt Lucija, in her slippers, asks him why he's crying. He says that he's remembering his life, Beethoven's, and that's why he's crying. Srečko winks at me. I see his mouth, his teeth with gaps between them, his fine hair and the remains of his tears because his eyes are red. My eyes get red when I cry, too. After, if I look at myself. He winks at me again. He's talking to me. To my face. I watch him, I look into his eyes. Srečko says that he can sing all Beethoven's compositions, for the orchestra, for the piano, symphonies, string quartets. He says he knows them all by heart. That it's all in his head and that when he gets lost and can't go on in a square, he remembers Beethoven, he says, and then he's less afraid of the wide square. I don't know what quartets are and all the rest. No one knows, I know.

I watch him, Srečko. The others laugh at him. They like it when he talks about Beethoven, because he cries, always. *Tata* says to him, Talk, talk, Srečko! But now he isn't talking anymore. Aunt Lucija says he has drunk too much, that's why he's crying, not because of Beethoven. I look at her slippers with the butterfly. I bend over and look under the table at her slippers. They really are just like mine.

I get up and go to the corner and stand on tiptoe. Oh, our Ballerina will dance, says *Tata*. Srečko walks into the yard. I see him come into the yard, I see him through the window in the kitchen. The others are sitting. Karlo says that soon they will unveil a monument in memory of the partisans who died. That the choir will sing. I don't know what a monument is and who partisans are. I stand on tiptoe. I look through the window. I see Srečko and his mama Lucija in her slippers. She's arranging his shirt, he's pushing her away, she tries to arrange his shirt again, he pushes her away. Then he lets her arrange his shirt.

Ivan. He's here. I see his head through the window. He'll come through the door now.

He's here. He's holding a bunch of flowers in both hands. Oh, how beautiful they are, says Elizabeta and puts her hands on her knees. Josipina gets up. OK, I'm going now. Wait, we'll have the cake now, says Mama. Ivan is here and we'll have the cake. Ivan is standing in front of me, still holding the flowers in both hands, looking upward at me. I look down at him, at his eyes. I look at his face. His hair is combed, he's wearing a white shirt and blue pants with a crease. Blue like the morning, when everything is blue. Josipina takes the flowers from him and pours water in a vase. Happy Birthday, Ballerina, says Ivan and shakes my hand. I'm not on my tiptoes now. I let him hold my hand. Mama cuts the cake. Josipina quickly eats a slice and says she's going. I can already see her—she'll run, with quick steps. She's off. I see her, Josipina is leaving.

I'm eating the cake with Ivan. Ivan is wiping my mouth with a napkin. He says I'm all chocolatey. How's school, Ivan? asks Karlo. Good, says Ivan, good, and he goes on eating the cake. Then *Tata* says something. What will you be when you grow up? A doctor, says Ivan. And then we eat our cake. Until we finish it.

Others are talking now. Ivan is with me, telling me he will cure me when he's no longer at school, when he's a doctor. I look at him and give him my hand. He takes it. He holds my hand. His hands are soft. Then he says he's going. Ciao, Ballerina, he says and leaves. Bye, Ivan, say hello to everyone at home, says Mama. And Ivan leaves, I see his head through the window.

In the evening, as we stand by the window, Mama says that Ivan is younger than me, that he's in second grade at college and that he's good at school. Mama also says that he doesn't live far away, next door, says Mama.

Karlo goes to the pantry. It's cold in the pantry. I know he's getting the accordion. Karlo plays the accordion. He's back. Mama is smiling, I see her.

For Ballerina, says Karlo and plays. Now Srečko and Lucija, his mama and my aunt, are here too. *Tata* is sitting. Everyone is looking at Karlo. Srečko is crying. Elizabeta is tapping her knees with her hands.

I stand on tiptoe again. I listen. Karlo is playing. The accordion. My toes are hurting. I grab a plate, squeeze it in my hand and hurl it at the door. Everyone ducks. The plate breaks. *Basta* for today, says Karlo and puts the accordion away. Srečko peers at me and leaves. Everyone walks into the yard, I see them. I take another plate and it breaks against the door. Mama is picking the pieces. Alright, alright, Ballerina, and she starts singing. Mama is singing.

Voolare, o, o! Cantare, o, o, o, o …

Now we're in the hall, both of us. We're holding hands and singing.

Nel blu, dipinto di blu, felice di stare lassù …

Mama has a nice voice. I can hear it even when she isn't singing, when she isn't talking. I hear it inside. She's holding my hand and singing. In the middle of the hall. She closes the door. Mama says it's the main door. Wait, she says. She closes it. I can't see the yard anymore. So that we don't disturb the neighbors, she says, and we go on singing, at the top of our voices, because the door is closed now. If Mama sings with me, I'm not afraid anymore.

She's holding my hand and walking me to the kitchen. We're singing. She walks me to the chair. I sit. I'm singing. Mama is stroking my shoulders, singing after me. I can't see her face, only the door. The hall. There's no light there. Mama puts a bundle of paper on the table. She says it's a magazine and I should leaf through it, she says. *Domenica del Corriere*, she says. I know she's already done this before. I know. *Domenica del Corriere*, she says, and I look through it. She says I should see what's happening in the world. So that you can tell me things, she says. I'm leafing through the magazine, singing. More quietly now. I look at the faces. Women's, men's. I don't know them. They've never been here. Then I stop looking. I look at the window. I can see them in the yard. They're all still there. They're looking into the kitchen. Elizabeta, Karlo, Srečko, Lucija, Ivan. Josipina isn't there. I know she ran away, I know she went through the door earlier.

In the evening Mama and I are standing by the window. There's a bed behind me. I know that Mama will take me to my bed. Soon. Now, we're here, by the window. Below is the yard, the chestnut tree, where the birds sleep. They're coming now. I see them. I can see the leaves moving. I look into the distance past the chestnut tree. Mama says there are fields, then come the hills and then the mountains. Mama says that there's a valley below the mountains and that that is where she was born, in that valley I can't see. Below the mountains. Mama is talking like she always does when we stand in front of the window and before she takes me to bed. Can you see? That's Mount Čaven, that's where the *burja* wind is born. And there, see? That is Angel Mountain, the blue one, see? I see. I say nothing.

That's where my nicest day was, she says. It was there. Early in the morning, Elizabeta and I walked. There, to Angel Mountain. We walked on the dewy grass, nearly two hours to the top. And suddenly, she says, we saw a meadow, big, huge, so that you couldn't see the end of it. And it was full of flowers. It was as white as snow … And then we walked among the flowers, Elizabeta and I, and we felt so good, I can't tell you how good, she says. Then we picked some flowers, a big bunch … And it was so nice, so terribly nice that I can't tell you how nice it was.

That's where my day is, she says, and takes me to bed. I lie down. Today was your day, Ballerina. Go to sleep now and don't start thinking. I feel her hands on my face. I look at her bending toward me. She kisses me. I can see the window behind her. I know the birds are sleeping, I'll go to sleep, too, and I will dream. Mama says I'll dream and everything will be alright.

2

I'm peeing, now. I can feel I'm peeing. I'm cold. I don't want to open my eyes, I don't want to look at the window. I can hear some footsteps. I know, Mama opens the door. I'm on the bed. I can hear her coming closer. Good morning, Ballerina, she says. We must change, it's a new day today. I know. I know very well it's a new day, because I wet myself, and because it's the morning. Mama is drying me. With a towel. It's rough. It hurts. Then she puts stockings on my feet. I know it's winter.

In the evening when Mama and I are standing by the window, the chestnut tree doesn't have leaves and the birds no longer sleep there. She's putting my stockings on, Mama, caressing my toes. Oh, my beautiful Ballerina, she says, we'll put some ointment on now, every night, on your toes, you know. Otherwise you won't dance anymore. Look, what they're like, they must hurt. And she strokes my toes, my feet.

I'm in the kitchen now. Sitting at the table. Looking at the door. *Tata* is in the hall, smoking and looking at the yard. The ash falls down. He stands and looks. Mama is breaking bread into a cup of coffee in front of me. I look at the milky coffee, I look at the bits of bread falling into it. I grab a spoon. I slurp. I chew, looking at the hall. *Tata* is looking at the yard. Then he takes his hat off the hook and puts it on. He looks in the mirror hanging on the wall. It's quiet. No one talks. He doesn't look at me. He steps out into the yard, I see him, he's leaving. To the bar, says Mama. I know he'll be home for lunch. I know I'll grab him by his ear. I'll hold it tight. First, I'll be in the corner, on tiptoes. I'll be tall, then it'll be lunch. And I'll hold his ear so that it hurts, later.

I hear footsteps. A woman is standing in the doorway. She's breathing deeply, quickly. I see Mama turn back. From the stove to the door. The woman doesn't say anything, just breathes. Then she says that Srečko phoned. That his mama was run over and is in hospital.

Mama is looking through the window at the yard. She doesn't

always look. Sometimes. Now. The table is laid for lunch. I'm standing in the corner, looking at Mama. I see her shoulders and her hair in a bun. She isn't moving, just looking through the window. Karlo walks into the kitchen now. Mama talks. The neighbor came to tell us that Lucija has been run over. Can you take me to Trieste after lunch?

I listen.

Yes, says Karlo. What's happened?

I don't know. She said Srečko phoned. He said that she's been run over. Karlo sits down at the table. I see *Tata* is coming. He's in the yard. He stops. He coughs, then comes in.

Lucija has been run over, Mama says. Karlo will take me to Trieste. Ballerina is coming with me.

I stand on tiptoe in the corner. *Tata* is standing in the door. He doesn't speak. He takes off his coat. His hat. He walks to the window. I know what he's doing. He's looking at the thermometer. It's only ten, he says. Then he takes a pencil from the top of the refrigerator. The pencil is always on top of the refrigerator and he takes it now. He writes something down. Mama says that he writes the temperature on a calendar. Every day. Then he turns on the Grundig to listen to the weather forecast. I know. Everyone is quiet then. Sometimes not, because I sing, but *Tata* says nothing. He turns off the radio and turns on the lights on the gondola. And then he looks at the gondola. And falls asleep at the table.

He's sitting now. I'm sitting, too. Karlo is looking at me. I know he's been in the woods. Mama says he guards the woods so that they're not cut down. Mama says he also looks after the animals in the woods so that they're not killed.

Mama is changing me. Karlo is also changing. *Tata* is in the kitchen. He's sleeping with his head on the table, holding his ear with his hand. I see him. From the hall. Mama dresses me, the dress with the butterflies. Then the coat. Let's go and see Aunt Lucija, she says. I look at the butterflies on the dress. Mama buttons up my coat. I can't see the butterflies anymore.

Karlo is driving the car. Mama says it isn't his. It belongs to the state. I don't know the state. I don't know who the state is. It has never been in our kitchen.

I'm sitting near Karlo. Mama is sitting behind me, I know. She put on a gray dress and a scarf on her head. I'm wearing the dress with butterflies. Karlo doesn't say anything. Neither does Mama. Now. I'm looking at the floor. I'm pressing my coat onto the dress so that the butterflies can't fly off. I see bits of branches. I see leaves. Dry leaves. On the ground. Then I look through the window. I have my hands on the glass. The road falls steeply down. I see houses running past. People on the road running past. I see them and then I don't see them anymore. They're behind me, I don't know where. Then I see other people, other houses. I'd stand on tiptoe. But I can't. I'd sing. I hear Mama. She's singing now. Just a little. Then she says: Don't be scared, Ballerina. We won't fall … All the roads in Trieste are like this … We're at the top, they're in Trieste …

Then Mama says quickly, Look, look there, can you see the sea … Can you see it, Ballerina?

I look. I see. I see a blue field. Like in the morning when Mama comes into the room and the chestnut tree in the yard is full of leaves.

Suddenly houses aren't running. People aren't running either. Karlo says we've arrived and that Lucija lives in that house. I look through the window. They don't see me. No one is looking at me. Karlo opens the door. He takes my hand. Come, Ballerina, he says. I'm standing in front of a tall house. I can't see the roof, there are no chestnut trees, there is no yard. Mama takes my hand. Let's go, Ballerina, she says.

Karlo opens a large door. He says it's made of iron. Let's see first if Srečko is home, he says. We go through the door. Mama is holding my hand. There's no light. I can only see it far away, the light. Then we walk on, toward the light. Karlo knocks on the first door. There is no light here. I see Srečko in the doorway. Suddenly the door is open and Srečko stands in front of us. I look at him. He says nothing. Then he says she died. He cries. We follow him. I look at the room. It's a big room. At one end I see two beds. A window on the other side. High up. You can't see through it. Below the window there is a washbasin, a closet and a chair.

Srečko is sitting on the chair. Karlo, Mama and I are sitting on the bed. Srečko is talking. I look at him and listen.

I told her to put her shoes on. She said she wasn't so stupid as to go in slippers. Mama, I said, those aren't shoes, they're slippers. No, no, she said. You're crazy, you can't even buy bread without getting lost in a square somewhere, you can't even get to Spain. Don't you talk to me. I know what slippers are. And she went. She forgot her bag and money, too. She's only getting some bread, I thought, she can go in her slippers. Then she said that she would come soon and that she would cook some pasta for me. Listen to some music, she said and left. She was crossing the road, they said, and lost a slipper. Then, they said, she turned round to go and get the slipper, but a car came and ran her over. The slippers were still there. I took them and cut them up. She didn't die immediately. When I telephoned, she was still alive. She told me to look after myself and not to leave the gas on because it was expensive and we didn't have money to waste, like others do. And then she died.

Srečko is quiet. Karlo says he will help him, if necessary, and Mama also says something. She says he should come to us if he needs anything. Srečko says nothing. I'm looking at his thin hair, his eyes that are red. His arms are hanging by his side as he sits there. I'm warm. I think of my dress with the butterflies. I feel even warmer. I'm afraid, suddenly, that the butterflies will suffocate. I get up, unbutton my coat, walk to the door, open it and go out, to the iron door, I walk faster, I open it, I walk on. I hear Karlo calling me. I walk on. People walk past me, now they look at me. I know they're looking at my butterflies. I don't want them to look at them. I want to be in the kitchen, in the corner, on my tiptoes, looking at the yard through the window. I want to sing. Karlo grabs my hand. Slowly, slowly, Ballerina, he says. Mama is here, too. You'll catch a cold, she says and buttons up my coat and the butterflies on my dress are covered again.

Again, houses are running past and people. Mama says I mustn't catch a cold because when I have a cold I don't sleep at night and I can't dream. That I break things then, if I don't sleep, that I pull everything out of the closet and throw it out into the yard and they have to shut me in the pantry then, even at night, like they did with grandad *Nono*, who is now in heaven. They shut him in the pantry, too, says Mama. I mustn't catch a cold. And if you don't calm down in the pantry, you have to go to Elizabeta's because I get so tired, Mama says. And if I can't stay at Elizabeta's those gentlemen in the car come and take me to hospital, Mama says. I know that. I see them. They stop in the door and smile. Then I go with them. And then, when they bring me back, Mama sings, I know she sings, because I can hear her, even there, where they take me. I hear her voice and I think she's there somewhere in the hall or the pantry, singing. Mama shuts herself in the pantry when they take me away, I know. I can see her shutting herself in there. I look into the kitchen from the yard and I see her. First she cries. When I'm shut away, I hear her sing, too.

Now it's evening. Mama and I are standing by the window. Mama says I should look at the stars, I should find my own star and give it a name. Then she talks. Poor Lucija, she says … She experienced so little good, always in that hole with no windows. Watching the door, all her life. Seeing who came and who left, taking in mail for the other people in the building and that's how it went. Silvester was nice. He played the organ in the church. Poor Srečko. What will happen to him, eh? What do you say, my beautiful Ballerina? And she takes me to bed. It's dark. I listen to her footsteps. They're moving away. Now I know my mama is in her room and that *Tata* is already asleep.

I WATCH HANDS. Mama's hands. They're caressing my toes. Each one separately. Now it's a new day. I'm already washed. Then we'll go down the stairs into the hall. She'll comb my hair. She's putting my stockings on now. She says they're woolen, they'll keep me warm. I know, whenever it's a new day, she puts my stockings on, because it's winter.

In the evening when we're standing by the window, Mama says that the birds haven't come yet, that they're far, where it's warm. I see them. On green trees. There are lots of them, in stockings. Birds. I watch hands. Mama's hands. She opens the door on the stove. She picks up a log. I see the fire, I see her hands with the log. She puts the log in the fire. She closes the door. She looks at the door, *Tata* is in the hall. He's combing his hair in front of the mirror. Mama takes a cup. She pours coffee. *Tata* comes into the kitchen, his hair combed. I go into the corner. I watch him. I see him slurping coffee and eating a piece of bread. He's quiet. First he combs his hair, then he drinks his coffee.

Mama goes to the pantry. I look at the door leading to the pantry, it's half open. I wait. I stand on tiptoe. I know Mama will come back from the pantry and close the door behind her. It's cold in the pantry. There's salami, cheese, butter and meat in there. Karlo buys meat in Sežana, I know. Mama says: Go across the border and get some meat. And Karlo goes, always. Then there's meat in the pantry, because it's cold there, colder than in the refrigerator, says Karlo. I'm looking at the door, it's half open. Mama is standing in the doorway to the pantry. I look at her hands. She's holding a bottle. She opens it. She takes out a glass. I know what she's going to do. She'll take some drops from the bottle and say: Here, Ballerina, drink this. And I'll drink. Then I won't stand on tiptoe for a while, I won't sing, I won't look at the yard. I won't know when Karlo will come from the woods or *Tata* from the bar.

Mama will give me the newspaper and I'll turn the pages back and forth and Mama will talk. That is Sophia Loren, that's Clark

Gable, Liz Taylor …

Tata is in the hall. With his hat. He says: I'm going to the bar. And he goes. I don't see him in the hall. I look at the faces, I go on looking. I don't know the faces. I see a woman in a long dress. The dress is white. She doesn't have a bow at the side. I look at her and I say nothing. Mama is behind me. I know she's behind me. She also looks at that face and then says: Greta Garbo. See how beautiful she is. When I used to come here for milk, she says, they had a cow. In the stable out there. And during the war as well. That was another cow then. We called her Greta. She had beautiful eyes. Just like Greta Garbo. Then Mama doesn't say anything else. I look at Greta Garbo. I look at her dress. White. She doesn't have a bow at the side. Greta Garbo only has a dress. Long and white.

We'll buy a television that's called Telefunken, says *Tata*. I see him. We've already eaten, earlier, after *Tata* returned from the bar and Greta Garbo was gone. I know we have eaten because I'm full. Next year, says *Tata* and goes to the hall. Oh yes, a television? says Karlo. He's looking at the hall. *Tata* turns around. I hear him speak. I listen. If they're going to the moon, we'll see it, too.

They won't go yet, says Karlo.

But you can see the whole world, if there's a television, says *Tata*.

Then we're quiet. What if we bought a toilet instead? says Mama. She smiles. She's beautiful, my mama, when she smiles.

They're holding me under the arms now. Mama on one side and Josipina on the other. Let's hurry, says Josipina, it's starting soon. Are you happy, Ballerina, to go for a little walk? And she caresses my hand.

We walk. Mama says the village is nice, even though it's cold. She says we're nicely wrapped up and won't be cold and that at the village hall it's also warm when there are lots of people. I look. I move and I look. I see the road, lights in the air. They shine onto the road. I see houses, windows, shops. Mama says that those are shops. Oooh, we've arrived, says Josipina.

Mama says we're in the village hall. I see lots of people. Mama undoes my coat. Josipina helps her. Then we sit down. In a row. People are sitting in rows, on wooden chairs. Everyone is looking straight ahead. I don't know them. They haven't been in our kitchen. I think I can see the postman. I can see his head. He's not wearing his cap. Mama says it's him. That he's wearing a tie. The postman is wearing a tie today, says Mama. He's good looking, isn't he? says Josipina. I see Mama nod. You'll see how beautiful it'll be, Ballerina, Josipina says, looking at the people. Josipina is looking at their heads. At the back of their necks. Then she says: There are lots of people. I'm happy when there are lots of people. Oh, look, the people I work for are here. They're all dressed up, aren't they?

Then it's dark. The only light is at the front, a bit higher up. I see a hole, full of lights. Then Josipina says that they'll come on stage now and I'll see how beautiful they are.

They're coming. People. I see them. They're coming into the light. One after another. They stand. Then another person comes. He bows and turns his back to the people sitting down, and waves his arms. The people standing in a line sing. They open their mouths. They're all looking at the man in front of them. He's waving his arms.

The people standing in a line are opening their mouths and singing. I look at a face on the left. In the light. He's opening his mouth. He's red. The man in front of him waves his arm. Then he stops. Suddenly. They stop singing. They have their mouths closed, now. Then the man in front turns toward us. I think that he's looking at me. That he can see me. I don't want him to look at me. He's tall. He has black hair and a tie. I don't want him to look at me. Mama and Josipina are clapping. The other people are doing it, too. Mama says I should clap as well.

I want to get up. I want to stand on tiptoe in the kitchen. Then I want to be by the window with my mama, looking at the yard. Mama is holding my hand. Look, see how nicely they sing, she says. And I see Ivan in the light. I know it's him. He's smaller. Ivan. I know he'll cure me. He speaks. I listen. He says: Dear guests, the choir has just sung a poem written by our great poet Prešeren. You've been listening to 'A Toast', set to music by Ubald Vrabec. The choir will sing the following songs. And he talks and talks. He's a good boy, isn't he?

says Josipina. Our little Ivan, says Mama. He talks and talks. Then he leaves. I want to see him. He isn't in the light anymore. He left. Then they sing. I don't want to listen. I think I'm in the kitchen, on tiptoe, high up. I see I'm there and I grab a glass and throw it at the door so that it breaks, and I see Mama sweeping it up. I'd like to hold my father's ear. Hold it hard. They keep singing. Mama sings better. I want Mama to sing. Now. I'll sing. Then she'll sing, too. Now. I want her to. My ears are ringing. I sing.

Vooolaree, o, o! Mama squeezes my hand. Not now, Ballerina, she says ... Not now ... I go on singing, *Can–taree, o, o, o, o* ... Josipina puts her hand on my mouth. Quiet, someone says. I don't know him. I get up, stand on tiptoe. I sing. *Nel blu, dipinto di blu ... Felice di–sta–re lassù* ... Let's go home, says Mama. I'm standing. I don't move. Mama and Josipina are dragging me behind them. I'm shouting. *O,o,o, Ooo!* They're all looking at me ... Silence, says someone ... Take her out! I hear someone else say. We're going, we're going, says Mama quietly. I can see she's red. It's warm, I think, *O, o, o, o.* Josipina is happy, she said so. Because there are lots of people. I know Josipina is happy because she said so. I'm happy, she said, when there are lots of people. I sing. I don't know where Ivan is. They drag me out, away, into the air. I breathe. I don't sing anymore. It's cold here.

We're standing by the window now. My mama and I. She says there are no stars, that there are clouds in the sky, that maybe it will snow. Then she says: A shame we didn't stay to the end, they sang so nicely, didn't they, Ballerina? I look through the window, into the darkness. Mama goes on: Josipina was happy. Let's go, Mama, tomorrow night I'm on my own, let's go to the concert. Let Ballerina come, too, she said. I'm on my own tonight. Giacomino will take the train at six, he's going home—to Bolzano—for a few days, she said ... At six I'll go to the watchmaker's, iron a few things and then I'll come. I'm so happy we're going to listen to the choir, she said ... Oh, Ballerina, Ballerina, it wasn't very nice, shouting like that ... It wasn't very nice. What will Ivan say, eh?

Now she isn't talking anymore. I see Ivan there in the light. Then

I don't see him any more. I listen. Mama is leaving. I hear footsteps in the kitchen. Karlo is there, I know. Sometimes he comes at night, unlocks the door, I hear the key, then he washes and goes to bed. I think I see Greta Garbo, her eyes. And I fall asleep.

4

THEY'RE HERE. In the tree. I hear them. The birds. The morning is blue. I look at the window, I look at the door of the closet, I look at my feet and my toes. It's a new day.

How quickly the years go by, says Mama. And our Ballerina will soon have a party. We'll buy a new dress, right? she says, caressing me. I'm still in bed. I look at her. Mama is blue, like before.

I'm standing in the kitchen, looking through the window at the yard. I hear footsteps. I know the postman is coming. I recognize them, his footsteps. I don't want him to come. Let him stay in the yard, I think. It's sunny there, he can stay in the yard, under the chestnut tree. I see him. He walks past the window, into the hall. The door is open. It's hot. I stand on tiptoe. The postman wipes his forehead with his sleeve. His face is red. Good day, Ivanka, he says and puts a letter on the table. He doesn't look at me. I stand on tiptoe and look at his face. Now he's not laughing. He's looking at his big bag and he's not laughing. It will happen like it always does. Mama will pour him a glass, he will drink, then he will open his mouth and I won't know whether he's suffocating or feeling good. Then he will laugh and talk. I don't like it when he talks. He knows everything, Mama says to me in the evening, by the window as we stand there, looking at the yard. He knows everything, says Mama. She's pouring his drink. The postman watches the glass filling. Then he picks it up, drinks it and opens his mouth. Mama and I look at his open mouth. I'm no longer standing on tiptoe. I'm in the corner, looking at his open mouth and his tightly shut eyes. Maybe he's in pain, I think. Something hurts. Mama is also looking at his eyes. She opens her mouth. She smiles. Then the mouth closes and the postman smiles. Now he starts to talk.

Hm-hm, a little drink is good for the heat … Eh, Ballerina? He looks at me now. I'm looking into his eyes. I think of Greta Garbo in the stable. That's what they say, Mama says as she turns to the stove, one glass does no harm in the heat. Then you don't sweat all day. The postman speaks again. I listen.

Have you seen, Ivanka, what they're doing over there?
Where?
Over there, in Vietnam …
Is there something new?
Yes, new … They're killing each other as usual …
Yes … They said on the radio that there are many dead.
I don't know when this war will end. They're all crazy!
That they are, says Mama and empties the boiling water into the sink under the window.

It steams. The postman again wipes his forehead with his sleeve.
OK, I must get on … Thanks for the drink … Bye, Ballerina.
And he leaves. I see him in the yard. I hear his footsteps. Then I can't hear them anymore. It's quiet. Mama isn't in the kitchen either. She's in the yard. Not long now before *Tata's* handkerchiefs are hanging on the line. Then I hear her call me.

Ballerina! Ballerina! Come out … Come and see … You've got a visitor!

I cross the kitchen to the door. The door is coming closer, the hall, the light from the yard, now I'm in the hall, looking through the front door at the yard, I go to the doorstep and then stop. Ivan.

Come, come, Ballerina, says Mama.

I don't move. I stand on the doorstep, looking toward Ivan. Ivan is there, near Mama, wearing short pants and a shirt with short sleeves. I'm also wearing a blouse with short sleeves. I'm not wearing stockings because it isn't winter, Mama says. Ivan has short hair and his ears are sticking out like they used to. Mama says I should go with Ivan. He'll take me for a walk.

I step onto the stair. First with one foot, then with the other. Ivan comes closer, takes my hand and says: Let's go, Ballerina!

And we cross the yard, under the chestnut tree where the birds sleep, then we turn toward the field where, Mama says, potatoes and beans are growing, planted by Karlo. The field is long. Ivan is silent. Then we come to a cherry tree and stop in its shade. We're looking at the field and Ivan is still holding my hand. I feel his little hand. I see him, I see him in the hall as he says he will cure me when he finishes school. Then I see him again here, under the cherry tree and

I feel his hand, his fingers. My hand is bigger. I could squeeze and crush his hand. I know he has no school now. Mama says Ivan isn't at school because it's summer. Maybe he'll cure me now, I think. We watch the field. Ivan is talking about beetles. He says that they learnt at school that beetles come and eat the potatoes. I'm scared. I think we won't have any potatoes left and we'll be hungry and will have to go to the moon, like the postman said. Then Ivan talks about some other beetles, which can only be seen at sunset. Ivan says they have pincers and they're black and that they're called long-horned beetles.

I look at the cherry tree. I look at its leaves, long and green. Mama says that the cherry tree is very old and that it will die soon. She says this sometimes, as we look out into the yard in the evening, standing in front of the window. She leans toward the glass and looks at it and then she always remembers her nice day on Angel Mountain, when she and Elizabeta picked flowers. A big bunch of them.

Now Ivan is holding my hand and we are walking in the tall grass. The field, the house and the yard can't be seen. Ivan says that we're going to the big valley, where it's cool and where there are many trees. We're still in the grass now and it reaches as high as Ivan's waist, to where I have a bow on my pink dress. Ivan says there are many daisies in the grass. I look at them. I'm thinking of Elizabeta and her tulips that she loves so much and she always says: Oh, how beautiful they are! And she puts her hands on her knees, when she says this. Always, when tulips are growing, Elizabeta says this and looks at them.

Ivan is no longer holding my hand. He's walking in front of me along a narrow path. I'm behind him. I look at his ears sticking out and his neck with the hair shaved off. Ivan has a thin neck. Mama says I have a thick neck, that I'm strong. I could take hold of his neck, Ivan's, I could grab it with both hands and lift him toward the moon. I forget his neck. I walk behind him, down the narrow sloping path, between two dry-stone walls. Ivan stops. We're here, he says and then walks on. I walk after him. I look at the meadow. I see that it's cut. I think someone must have cut it with big scissors. Josipina has scissors like that at home. Maybe she cut it. She says she cuts material with the scissors and then makes clothes for herself. I know that because she once talked about it with Mama in our kitchen. I don't know why Josipina cuts meadows with those scissors. Karlo says that you must look after your tools otherwise they break.

Where Josipina cut the meadow, the valley starts, a big valley. Ivan says that it's the biggest valley and that lots of trees grow in it. We walk on. The slope is steep now. The path is narrow and full of soil. Make sure you don't fall, says Ivan and walks on. I see butterflies, suddenly. Lots of butterflies, as blue as the morning, as blue as Mama when she opens the door and looks into my room. Then she's blue from the morning, from the butterflies. I look at the butterflies and walk behind Ivan. They're like the ones on my dress. I'm afraid they may be the same ones. Mama sometimes leaves the closet open and I'm always scared when the closet is open because the butterflies could escape into the room, then down the stairs to the hall, into the kitchen, and then they may hit the window, wanting to fly into the yard. Butterflies don't know what a door is. Mama says that we can go out only through a door, an open door. I know that. Butterflies don't know it. But if it's them, if the butterflies flying around me now are my butterflies, it means they didn't fly into the window, they found the door and if they found the door they will come back through it again. In the evening they will be in the closet again, on my dress. If the door is open.

Ivan says I should sit down. He's already sitting on a stone. I sit. He takes my hand and tells me to look how many trees there are in the valley. I lift my eyes, look at the branches and, through them, at the patches of the sky. Then Ivan tells me the names of the trees. He points at them with his finger: Ash, beech, oak, mahaleb cherry, acacia … Ivan says that he has learnt these names at school and that I will learn them, too, when I go back to school, after he has cured me. Ivan says that those are tree trunks, thick, thin, twisted. Look at that one, he says, how thick it is . . . I'm happy Ivan is talking. Then I look at him. He breaks a blade of grass next to the stone and says we'll look for a cricket.

He's no longer holding my hand. He bends lower down and says: See the hole? There's a cricket in there. He's asleep now. I'll wake him and we'll take him home. You have to tickle it, like this, in and out, with a bit of grass. I look at him. I look at the hole in the ground and the blade of grass going in.

Ivan isn't talking anymore. Then, suddenly, he says, Look at him! He brings his hands, squeezed together, to my face. He's holding something. I see little legs between his fingers. The legs are moving. A cricket! says Ivan. It's ours now. Let's go home. We'll put him in a box. He goes. I walk behind him. I see him, holding his hands together. It feels as if I can see the little insect in his hands, how it wants some light, how it wants out. I'm scared. Then Ivan stops. We're already in the tall grass. He says he has to pee, that he can't last any longer, that the cricket is tickling him so much he has to go pee. He tells me to open my hands and look after the cricket. I'm scared. I don't understand what it means to look after the cricket. Ivan says to open my hands so that he can put the cricket in there because he has to pee. I don't know why he has to pee without the cricket. Ivan laughs, talks louder. I feel I would like to stand on tiptoe and sing. I'm scared. Then I see my hands in front of me. They are opening, my hands, opening wide. Ivan comes closer, puts his closed hands onto my hands and says I should close them immediately so that the cricket doesn't escape. And he drops the cricket. I see my hands covering each other and feel the small legs in them. It tickles. I know I'm looking after the cricket. I stand and look at my hands, then I lift my eyes and see Ivan. He says he's peeing. Karlo pees like this, too, standing up and *Tata* does as well. I know. Mama says I can't pee standing up, I have to sit on the toilet. Or in bed, every morning, I can pee in bed. I'm lying down then. I never do it standing up. When it's morning and I wet myself and Mama washes me and changes my clothes and says it's a new day. I'm holding the cricket in my hands, looking at Ivan. He's coming closer, with his ears sticking out. He's small. The grass still reaches up to his waist. I feel I'm tall. Mama says I'm tall. Then Ivan says: Hold it well, so that it doesn't run away, you can put it in a box and then you can listen to it in the evening, going chirp-chirp.

We walk on. Then we stop under the cherry tree at the end of the field. You go home on your own now! says Ivan. You're a big girl, he adds and leaves. I see him running along the path, far away. I don't know why I'm alone under the cherry tree with the cricket. He said

I was a big girl. That's what Mama says, too, she's always saying that. When I'm breaking plates and glasses, throwing them at the door, Mama says, Ballerina is a big girl and shouldn't be doing this, we must behave nicely.

Now I'm alone under the cherry tree with a cricket in my hands. I can't go on. I look at the tree top. I see ants on the trunk, walking up. I want to climb up, too. I stand on tiptoe so that my toes hurt. It seems I'm even bigger then. My toes always hurt when I do this. I'm scared. I sing.

Marina, Marina, Marina,
ti voglio al più presto sposar,
o mia bella mora, no, non mi lasciare,
non mi devi rovinare,
o no, no, no, no, nooo!

The cricket sits still in my hand. Maybe it's not breathing. I don't know, I daren't look. I sing even louder. It seems to me that I can hear Mama sing. I can't see her, it just seems like she's singing, like always, because she knows I'm scared whenever I sing. Then I shout. I'm standing on tiptoe under the cherry tree. I know I have a cricket in my hand, that I will put it in a box later, even if it isn't breathing anymore. She'll bury it. Mama. She'll do a funeral and Ivan will come. Together we will bury the cricket, if it stops breathing. And then Ivan will make a wreath of daisies for the cricket. If it's dead. I don't want it to be dead. I'm scared. I sing even louder. Now I see her. Mama is coming. She's coming along the field, coming closer. She's singing, I can hear her. We're both singing. Me under the cherry tree, her by the field in which potatoes and beans are growing. Then she comes. Now she's here, I feel her caressing me, talking to me. Alright, alright, Ballerina … Come, it's alright now. I'm not standing on tiptoe anymore, I'm not singing. I'm still holding the cricket in my hands. Then we will come into the yard, then into the hall and the kitchen and I'll be there, in the corner, looking through the window toward the yard and Mama will take the cricket and put it in a box, as always when Ivan leaves me under the cherry tree. Mama says Ivan is joking, that he did this last summer, too. I don't know what last summer is.

Now it's evening. Mama and I are standing by the window in the room. Behind me is the bed. Mama will take me there, later, and she'll tell me to rest because it's been a long day, and that I should have sweet dreams.

We're looking at the yard and the sky behind it. Mama says there are many stars and if I see a star falling toward the earth, I should make a wish. She says that she always wishes for her nicest day, that she was once again on Angel Mountain, alone or with Elizabeta. Just once more, she says. Then she leans out of the open window and looks at the cherry tree. I see that she's looking at the cherry tree at the end of the field. Then she says: When you were very little and it was the war, we dug a hole near that cherry tree so that we were able to hide from the bombs. We all hid. Karlo, Josipina, Srečko, when he was here, God knows what will happen to him, and *Tata*. Once we hid because the alarm sounded and then we were all very quiet in the hole under the cherry tree. We heard airplanes and suddenly there was a bang. We were startled and you began crying. But it wasn't a bomb. *Tata* had a bottle with him. Of champagne. The bang sounded like a bomb. God only knows where he found the bottle. Maybe at the place where the Germans were. Occasionally he chopped wood at the German barracks. They paid him a little and gave him some food. And he played cards with the cook, who knows, maybe he won that bottle. He never told me. Then we drank as the real bombs were falling. There, in that hole under the cherry tree. *Tata* looked like Uncle Feliks, who's already gone to heaven. Uncle Feliks was a partisan. But he didn't shoot. He only drew on walls, wherever partisans went. On houses. He drew Tito and wrote *Long live Yugoslavia*. He had nice handwriting. Once he drew Tito with a moustache and then he was no longer a partisan. He was nothing. Like *Tata*. Poor Feliks. You were ever so little. You didn't know him, Uncle Feliks. He went to heaven very soon, the poor thing. Then Mama stops talking. All she says is: Oooh, let's go to bed.

Then I lie there. I don't know where the cricket is. Mama says it's in a box. I don't know who Uncle Feliks is, who Tito was and who is *Long live Yugoslavia*. I haven't seen it in our kitchen yet.

5

I'M LYING IN bed, covered. I don't know when Mama covered me. I look at the window. No light. I see the moon in the window. Mama says it's getting fatter. I see Mama in the window. How time flies, she says, and I don't see her anymore. I know that soon I won't see the moon and there'll be light and a new day. Now there's no light yet. Now there's the window. There's the moon getting fatter. I listen to Mama. I hear her words. Once, when she stood by the window with me and talked. Srečko gets his mother's pension, she said. Although it's not much, at least he has enough to eat. I just hope he doesn't get lost, poor Srečko. He's already walked to the station, said he would get a train and go to Vienna. He went to the station, carrying the bag he takes to buy bread, saying he would go to Vienna. Karlo met him and told him he couldn't go to Vienna with his bread bag. Who knows what he would do there. In Vienna, so far away, with all those streets and squares and a bread bag.

Now I can't hear her words. I do hear footsteps on the stairs. I hear them clearly. Each one of them. On the stone stairs. I know it's Karlo. He has woken up. He's awake like me. He isn't coming to my room. He's going downstairs. Mama says that Karlo sometimes gets out of bed when the moon is out and goes for a walk. He goes to the kitchen, then into the hall and out into the yard, then he walks over the field where potatoes and beans are growing. Mama says she hears him leave his room in the attic and walk down the stairs to the hall, the yard, the field. When will you fix that hole of yours in the attic? says Mama when she's angry. Mama says that Karlo sleeps in a hole and that he's big enough to turn it into a home. He's also got a job, says Mama, in the woods. He's earning money and could fix the house, or at least paint it white. Mama wants the walls in the house white, the windows white and the doors white. *Tata* says it doesn't matter. And Mama is sad. I know, because she goes to the pantry, into which they used to shut *Nono* when he was drunk and making a racket. Buy some paint, says Mama to Karlo as we sit at the table and *Tata* is coughing in the hall. We'll paint everything white, she says.

But Karlo says nothing. Like now. I hear him in the kitchen, in the hall. He's opening the door now. Mama says he sleeps and walks, and that he mustn't wake up quickly. That he has to wake up slowly, like a child, says Mama. I want to see him. I want to go to the window and look into the yard. I get up. As I'm getting up I think of Ivan. Mama says that it's been a few years now since Ivan came to visit us. But I see him. I think of him and see him. Whenever I'm getting up from my bed. Alone. When Mama isn't here, I see Ivan. Mama says he's in school in Ljubljana now, that he will soon come back. I think he'll cure me and then we'll go to school together. I see him, he's small, his ears stick out and he's wearing shorts and the grass is tall. I always see him when I get up alone.

I'm up now. I look at the window. I go closer. I see the moon moving closer, and the window. The window with the moon. Now I'm here, I see the tree top where the birds sleep. I see the chestnut tree. I see the field and, further away, the cherry tree. The moon is shining onto the field and the cherry tree. I see Karlo. I see him. He's walking by the field, like Mama says. He stops. I'm standing by the window, looking. At him standing by the field. I hear Mama talking to me by the window. She's not here, but I can hear her. Mama says she would like to go to Karlo sometime and listen to what he's saying, because he's always talking, says Mama, when he gets up and the moon is shining. Mama also says that Karlo talks about all the things he doesn't want to tell her when he's awake. Mama says that Karlo is the only other healthy person in the house and they should talk more.

I want to go down the stairs, into the yard, to Karlo. I want to listen to what he's saying. Mama isn't there. She's asleep. So is *Tata*. I hear him snoring. Mama says she likes *Tata* snoring because it is like then, when she was told to wait for Franc, that he was handsome and that she would marry him. And then we married, Mama says sometimes, because he came and he was handsome and we married and he snored, *mamma mia*, how he snored, the poor thing. I'm walking toward the door, I go through the door, onto the stairs. The moon is there. Shining. A little, only just. I see my bare feet on the stairs. Now I'm in the hall. The door to the yard is open, I see the yard, the moon. I walk through the yard toward the field. I see him. He's there. Standing by the field, not moving. I watch him. I go closer. I see him ever closer. Now I'm nearly next to him. I'm not afraid of anything. Karlo is my brother. He drives me places. Drives me to Elizabeta's. He's good, he guards the woods, the trees and the animals, says Mama, he just needs to buy the paint so that we can paint the house and he must fix that hole he sleeps in and paint it white. I stand and watch him. I'm cold now. There's no Mama to cover me. There's Karlo. He's my brother. I listen. I don't hear him. I can see his lips move, but I don't hear anything. Karlo is talking. He doesn't talk in the kitchen. I don't hear him now. His lips are moving, but I can't hear what he's saying. I want him to see me, I want to hear him. I want to wake him. I mustn't. Mama says he must be woken up slowly. I'd run into him and send him to the woods, to guard the animals and trees, to get the paint so that we can paint the house, the walls, the windows and the doors. I'm looking at him. He isn't looking at me. He's looking at the field in which potatoes and beans are growing, and his lips are moving. Then he says: Feliks! I hear very clearly. He says Feliks! A number of times.

Uncle Feliks. He's in heaven, I know. Mama says Uncle Feliks is already in heaven, and she points at the clouds as she says this. Karlo is talking to him, I think. He's not here, the uncle. Only Karlo is here, talking and looking at the field and talking to Feliks. I think Uncle Feliks has come from heaven, he's there, where Karlo is looking, in the field among the beans. I don't know who Feliks is, I don't know what his ears look like, what his eyes look like and what his legs look like. Mama says that he went to heaven early, that I didn't know him, that I was very little. Maybe he's different now, Uncle Feliks, and Karlo knows what he's like. Karlo is my brother. He's looking at the field, talking to Uncle Feliks. I don't hear the uncle, either. I look into the beans and I don't hear him. I want to hear. I want to hear Uncle Feliks. I want him to talk to me, to tell me things. I feel the wind now. I'm cold. I want to hear him, Uncle Feliks, telling me about what Mama says. I want him to tell me, see, Ballerina, how nicely I write ... Look, Ballerina, how beautifully I can draw. I want him to write *Long live Yugoslavia*, I want him to write *Our Tito*, I want him to draw the partisans, I want him to draw Tito with a moustache, and afterward, if he wants, he can go back to heaven. I move closer to Karlo, I want to wake him so that he tells me who Uncle Feliks is, I want him to tell Uncle to talk louder, to shout if he wants, to sing because there's no one, not even light, the moon is still up there and Karlo is here, by the field! No one else would hear him. Just the two of us. Me and Karlo. I want that now! I run into Karlo. Karlo shakes and looks at me. I see his eyes. I think he's scared, he opens his mouth. He shouts, Balleriiinaaaa!! I watch him. I'm scared. I don't know anymore if my brother Karlo is the one standing in front of me. He's holding his head and walking along the field, he trips and falls, gets up, walks toward the house, then he stops, looks at me, I'm standing, feeling cold … He's getting closer, he's here. He takes my hand, pulls me. He says that it's the fall, that I will get a cold … Come, Ballerina. Then I see lights in the house. I hear Mama's voice. She's calling me, Balleriiinaaa! Balleriiinaaa! She must be in the yard. Yes. I see her. Karlo is pulling me, then he lets go of me in the yard and walks into the house. Mama puts her arms around me. Where have you been, Ballerina? she says. I told you that Karlo must be woken up slowly. You see what he's like. He has to go to work tomorrow and now he won't be able to sleep. Oh, my Ballerina, Ballerina … Come, she says and leads me into the house.

I don't want to go to bed. I don't want to go to the kitchen. Mama is holding my hand. I'm looking at the moon. I don't want to go into the house. I'm looking at the tree top in which birds are sleeping, I'm looking at the window of my room, Mama and I are standing in front of it, looking at Angel Mountain, then we're nearly in the hall, I'm looking at the oleanders in front of the door, Mama says they're poisonous, but very beautiful. Mama says oleanders are white, their blossoms are as white as the doors, the walls, the windows when they've been painted. She's pulling me up the stairs. To my room. Come, Ballerina, you'll lie down now and dream … Come!

I don't want to. I take a pillow and throw it at the window, I go to the closet, take my dresses, throw them on the floor, I go to the window, Mama is trying to catch me, I throw the pillow through the window, I throw the clothes through the window, I pick up the chair. Inside, where Mama says my heart is, it hurts, badly. Then my ears ring. I want to stand on tiptoe, I want to sing, but I can't. I feel my mouth opening and screaming, now, screaming at the top of my voice. I know *Tata* will wake up. I know, Karlo will come, too. I scream, I don't want to sleep, I don't want Mama, I don't want anybody … I see Mama, now she'll go to the pantry for the drops. She'll give me the drops and then she'll shut me into the pantry, and she'll cry when Karlo drives me to Elizabeta's. I'm screaming. *Tata* comes. Mama says: Franc, help, and she's crying, I know she's crying. Karlo is already in the yard. I know, like always. He's picking up the pillow, the clothes. I'm holding the chair and turning it around so that no one comes close. Franc, help, says Mama. *Tata* is standing in the door, wearing big pajamas, he's looking at me, he doesn't say anything, for a long time he doesn't say anything, then he comes closer, I see him. He's right next to me. I know he has come so that I could grab him by the ear, so that I could pull his ear and it would hurt him. He's looking at me. I grab his ear. I twist his ear. Mama isn't here anymore. I know she's getting the drops ready. I'm twisting the ear and pulling it. *Tata*, wearing his pajamas, is nearly stumbling, but he's letting me drag him to the stairs, to the hall, to the kitchen.

Now it's light. Morning. Mama is blue again. My mama is beautiful when it's morning. She's sitting at the table. I've already had the drops. I'm standing in the corner of the kitchen. *Tata* is sitting at the table. He's turned on the lights on the gondola, he's looking at the gondola with the lights and sitting at the table. I can hear footsteps, Karlo is coming down the stairs. I'm not screaming anymore, I'm not standing on tiptoe, I'm not singing. I'm dressed in my pink dress, the one with the bow. I don't understand why everyone is in the kitchen so early. The morning is blue, even in the kitchen. We're all blue from the morning. Karlo stands in the doorway. I can see him holding a bag in his hand. I think of the moon and the field and of Uncle Feliks in heaven. *Tata* is still looking at the gondola with the lights. Karlo is standing in the doorway with the bag. Then Mama says I'm going to Elizabeta's, that she's tired and must have a rest. She puts her arms around me, I feel her cheeks, her bony cheeks on my face. Then she goes to the pantry and cries. I go to Karlo. I always go on my own, when Mama tells me I'm going to Elizabeta's. I see *Tata* looking at the gondola. He says: Be good, Ballerina. And I go through the door to the hall, next to the oleanders, out to Elizabeta's.

6

ELIZABETA IS coming toward me. Just like before. I know it's like always when Karlo brings me to her house when Mama is tired and crying in the pantry with the door closed. Elizabeta is coming toward me. She's walking along a narrow path covered with little stones. I'm standing on the stones and holding a bag in my right hand. I can feel the small stones under my toes, I can feel them through the soles of my shoes. I know I'm wearing slippers with a bow, because my toes hurt less if I wear slippers with a bow, just like Aunt Lucija did when she was run over by a car. Mama says that she's in heaven, too. I can see her up there in the clouds, in her slippers with a butterfly. I don't know if her toes hurt, too, up there in heaven. Mama says that it's nice in heaven, that we are happy if we go to heaven. Mama is always saying that as we stand by the window. She says we'll all go there, to heaven, even Karlo, if he buys some paint and paints the door white.

I look at Elizabeta. I think she's Mama because she's like Mama. Even her hair, eyes, nose and mouth are the same. And she walks like Mama and laughs like Mama, only her voice is different. Come, Ballerina, she says, taking my bag in one hand and leading me by the other along the narrow path toward her house.

I can feel the stones, every one of them. Elizabeta says that there are as many little stones on the path as there are drops of rain in the worst possible downpour. Oh, so many little stones, she says, as we walk toward her house. She always says this when I visit her and we walk along the path. Then she says, laughing: Mrs. Sprigge knew how many there are, she counted them all before they took her home. Elizabeta says they took her to England.

I know who Mrs. Sprigge is. As Mama and I stand by the window, looking toward Angel Mountain, she tells me how she and Elizabeta came to Trieste, no older than little girls, and they washed and ironed and cleaned other people's houses. Mama says that Elizabeta talks nice, that I can learn a lot from her because she has read many books and that was why she got a job with Mrs. Sprigge, who came from England and was married to a rich gentleman. Mama says that, at first, Elizabeta looked after the plants in the greenhouse and then she started cooking and cleaning and ironing. Josipina, too, learnt how to iron from Elizabeta, Mama says, and if she didn't have to hide from Giacomino she could be the best ironing woman in Trieste, Mama says.

Elizabeta is still holding my hand. The path covered with little stones is very long because the garden is very big and the trees are big and the house in which Mrs. Sprigge used to live is also big. Aunt Elizabeta's house is small, there at the end of the path covered in little stones that Mrs. Sprigge counted before they took her back to England. Mama says that Mrs. Sprigge left that little house to Aunt Elizabeta until she dies, that now the little house belongs to Elizabeta and only to her until it is time for her to go to heaven, Mama says.

I look at the tall trees. Elizabeta says that they're poplars and spruces. I look at the wooden benches dotted around among the flower beds, where Mrs. Sprigge and her husband used to sit, says Elizabeta, and I walk on the little stones toward the little house at the end of the path. Elizabeta says that I will see squirrels and woodpeckers, those yellow ones, Elizabeta says. She's telling me that squirrels aren't afraid of anyone, that they come every year at the same time and take walnuts from your hand. Like this, says Elizabeta, you stretch out your hand, open it and put a nice, fat walnut on it, and a squirrel comes hopping along, looks at you, takes the nut, looks at you again and then climbs into one of the spruces.

Mama says that Elizabeta always had it very good at Mrs. Sprigge's. When Mrs. Sprigge had guests, Elizabeta cooked for them, when cleaning had to be done she cleaned, when the garden needed watering she watered it, when, in the winter, the heater in the greenhouse had to be turned on she turned it on, when Mrs. Sprigge called her in the middle of the night using a special electric bell installed in the little house at the end of the path covered with little stones Elizabeta went and told her nice stories, if Mrs. Sprigge felt lonely or scared in the big house after her husband Mr. Sprigge died, immediately after the dog called Havy.

Elizabeta is still holding me by the hand. Now we are climbing the stairs to her house, hers until she dies. I look back. I always look back, I know. Havy always used to come up the stairs when I was at Elizabeta's and Mama said: She doesn't speak. She just stands on tiptoe, singing. They say it happens to children sometimes. The dog came running with his big mouth and licked me and I laughed because it tickled. And then Elizabeta always closed the door on the veranda and said that Havy had to stay outside. Mama says that Elizabeta can speak English because Havy always understood her when she told him to *seet daun* or *kam hir*. Mama says that Elizabeta even used to pick up his poop around the garden and put it in the dustbin behind her house. Mama says that Elizabeta is alone now, that Mrs. Sprigge went back to England after she had counted all the stones in the garden, that her big house and garden are being sold, that Elizabeta only looks after the flower beds and the greenhouse now because she wants to. Elizabeta says that the garden has to look nice, without weeds, and that the path with little stones always has to be raked. Mama says that Elizabeta has been in that little house for thirty years and more and that she is used to it and that that is right.

It's raining. I'm sitting next to the bed and I can see the window. Outside is the garden, big, with big trees, squirrels, flower beds and benches on which Mrs. Sprigge used to sit. I don't know why Karlo has brought me to Elizabeta's. In the past, often, and now today, when it's raining and Elizabeta says that it will be winter soon, that it's very cold already and I must wear stockings, as Mama says. Elizabeta says that I'll stay here while Mama has a break. You'll have a good time here, Ballerina, you'll see. You know that you always have a good time with me, says Elizabeta. I know she also has the drops in the old refrigerator given to her by Mrs. Sprigge after she bought a new one. I can see her opening the fridge and taking out the bottle of drops. Then I know that I'll be looking through the window and I won't know where the garden is, where the trees with squirrels are and where the benches that Mrs. Sprigge used to sit on are. Elizabeta says I should leaf through magazines. She's like Mama. I'm holding a magazine on my lap and leafing through, Elizabeta is standing behind me. Like Mama. And she's talking. She says: Oooh, look at that, how beautiful she is … and she points to a young lady in a long dress. I think it's

Greta Garbo. Elizabeta says it's Gina Lollobrigida and that the man next to her is a film actor and that he's very handsome, she says …

And then I'm still here, at Elizabeta's. Elizabeta also says that time flies. She says nothing about the moon, Elizabeta, she says nothing about Vietnam like the postman, we don't stand by the window, looking toward Angel Mountain that my Mama loves so much. Elizabeta says that it's as peaceful here as it is where angels are and that she will be happy if her life ends like this some time and she goes to heaven to Aunt Lucija and Uncle Feliks.

I open my eyes. My room at Elizabeta's is as blue as my Mama. I have wet myself. I know. I'm cold. Elizabeta washes me. There are no steps, no hall, just the veranda and then the garden with the tall trees. I can see it, through the window, as she is washing me in the bathroom. Then she combs my hair, sits on the edge of the bath, puts her hands in her lap and says: Oooh, how beautiful she is, our Ballerina.

I'm looking at myself in the mirror in front of the veranda, a narrow mirror in the middle of the coat rack. I can see that Elizabeta has dressed me in a brown dress with buttons and a thick top. Then I see a face that I know is mine. Elizabeta says that I always laugh when I'm standing in front of that mirror. She says I'm happy because I'm laughing and I think that it's true what Elizabeta says, as there is also the field in that mirror, and the potatoes that need digging so that the soil can rest and smell nice, as Mama says, but she is not there. And I look at the field and I think that it smells nice because it will be dug up. I see Mama bending over the field to give it a drop of perfume on which it says Mennen and which is aftershave, Mama says, but it's like perfume. Then Elizabeta says it's draughty, that she will close the veranda door. And I'm no longer there in the mirror. Her scarf with red flowers and her coat are hanging on the rack and below the mirror there's an umbrella, a big black umbrella. I know *Tata* has an umbrella like that and Karlo sometimes takes it when there is a storm. I think Karlo has come to take me home, that Mama has had her break. I can't see him. All I can see is me, the coat, the flowery scarf and the umbrella. Elizabeta says I'm beautiful. Then she says that if I'm good she will tell me a nice story in the evening, like the ones she used to tell Mrs. Sprigge when she was scared of the big house and felt lonely. Elizabeta makes my breakfast, as always when it's a new day. Then she will go in the garden and plant tulips. Elizabeta says that tulips have to be planted before the winter, they do better that way. Then she will cook my lunch, give me a magazine and in the early evening we will go to the greenhouse to talk to the flowers, she'll say. It's nice when Elizabeta talks to the flowers. I think that I'm in that big valley and that Ivan is with me, telling me the names of trees, that we are walking in the tall grass, catching crickets and that Mama is singing.

We're in the garden now. Elizabeta is bent over, pushing tulip bulbs into the soil. I can see her back, her hair in the bun on her head, just like Mama's. Above me are trees, poplars and spruces, and the sun. Autumnal, says Elizabeta, breathing with difficulty, as she is pushing tulip bulbs into the soil. Then she turns toward me. Her face is red and sweaty and she is smiling. Mrs. Sprigge loved tulips, she says, and turns back to the soil. Then she moves to where there are no tulip bulbs yet. Elizabeta says that there are nearly three thousand of them, and each year she buys a few more because some dry up and don't flower, even when you plant them with all your love. And then they need watering, even in the autumn, says Elizabeta.

Afterwards, we sit on the bench where Mrs. Sprigge used to sit, alone or with her husband. We look at the closed windows of the big house in which Mrs. Sprigge used to live, we look at the flower beds with the newly planted tulip bulbs, we look at the trees. It's windy. Elizabeta says it's blowing from the south because sirens from ships can be heard. She says that the gentleman Mrs. Sprigge was married to had many ships that sailed all over the world. Oh dear, how many times he used to say that we would take a boat far away, to Australia, says Elizabeta and smiles at me. I can see her face. It's very close. I can see her eyes, they're green. Mama says that Elizabeta has such green eyes, like a river in the sun. I can see her eyes fill with tears. Mama says that when there are tears in them Elizabeta's eyes are like a river after rain.

Now I know as I look at Elizabeta, at her face, I know I'm standing by the window with my Mama. It is evening and together we are looking at the garden, toward the field and the cherry tree and Mama says: Mrs. Sprigge knew that they loved each other, Elizabeta and her husband, she knew that Elizabeta often cried because of it, and she used to comfort her, she was always comforting Elizabeta. Then he died and Mrs. Sprigge started counting the little stones in the garden and then they came from England to get her. Poor Elizabeta, poor Mrs. Sprigge.

Now I see Elizabeta again. She's walking among the flower beds, examining them. I'm sitting on the bench. Elizabeta is walking toward the house. She comes to a large, green bush. I can't see her anymore. I'm sitting on the bench and I can't see her.

Elizabeta says it will soon be evening and that we have to measure the temperature in the greenhouse. She says I've been very good, so far, and that later she will tell me a nice story. Later, she says, when it's evening.

I'm wearing a top like in the morning, like I've always worn since the beginning, and it is the fall and Elizabeta and I are going to the greenhouse. Nearby, a few yards from her house, says Elizabeta. She's wearing a coat, too. She says it'll be a harsh winter and the plants must be prepared for it.

Three steps down. It's quiet. The sky has cleared and through the glass of the greenhouse I can see stars. At the end of the aisle dividing the greenhouse into two equal parts, there is a thermometer and here, near the door, a heater. I watch. Elizabeta is telling me the names of the plants. On the right, there are geraniums, she says, because Mrs. Sprigge so loved to see them on her terrace. Then Elizabeta says nothing. She looks at the thermometer, walks among the plants, whispering something. I can't understand what she is saying. Now Elizabeta is like Karlo when he talks to Uncle Feliks and I can't understand him. Then she looks up. Look at the clouds, she says, can you see? They're bringing winter. Then she's silent again. I'm standing by the door, looking into the greenhouse and Elizabeta in it. Suddenly she stops, looks at me and says: Look, Ballerina, come closer, look! I think that Elizabeta wants to show me a squirrel I have already seen once before. It stopped, looked at me, took the nut, looked at me again and climbed into a spruce. Then I go closer. I look at her and see only a small part of her face. Everything is green. I can see Elizabeta covered with greenery. I can see her eyes, they're green. I come to her, my ears are whistling, loudly, so loudly. I want to sing with my Mama. I stand on my tiptoes. Elizabeta says: Look! And she shows me a ray of light on a geranium leaf. It's reflecting from the glass on the roof, she tells me. Like a ray from heaven, she says and turns away. Let's go, she says, it'll soon be dark and I have to tell you a story. I look at her leaving the greenhouse and suddenly I don't see her anymore. I step on tiptoes, look at the sky through the glass and I don't sing. You do that, you look, says Elizabeta. I can hear her like I always do when I stay in the greenhouse and evening is near.

7

AND THEN I dream. I'm walking along a path covered in gravel. Greta Garbo comes the other way and far away I see Gina Lollobrigida, wearing my dress with butterflies. I'm walking toward her, past Greta Garbo, who looks at me with her big eyes and says: Ciao, Ballerina! I hurry toward Gina Lollobrigida and she opens her arms wide. I think she wants to hug me, I know I must get to her quickly, because she hasn't got much time, Gina. I'm rushing. My toes are hurting, I'm going as fast as I can, I'm already with her, only a little more and I'll be able to touch her. Suddenly Gina Lollobrigida rises from the earth. I look up and stop. Gina is flying high into the sky, wearing my dress with butterflies. I'm breathing deeply, looking up into the air, soon I won't be able to see her. I can feel it, I know. She's gone. I'm still looking at the sky. Then I see bits of paper falling to the earth. They're flying and falling down. They're heavy. As they hit the ground, they make a lot of noise, the ground shakes and I with it. I want to pick up one of the bits of paper. I can't find any. There's just a big hole. I look into it. I see Srečko in it. Ciao, Ballerina, he shouts, waving his arms. Come with me, he shouts, come with me so that I don't get lost. Then, on the other side of the big hole created by a bit of Gina Lollobrigida, I see Lucija. Aunt Lucija, I say, look down, Srečko is there, he hasn't got lost. Aunt Lucija looks at me. Then comes Uncle Feliks. He's small, with big ears and a pointy nose. Uncle Feliks, I say, look, Srečko is down there, he's not lost ... Then Aunt Lucija says: Ballerina, you're even worse than Srečko, look, can't you see you're barefoot? And I look and see that I'm barefoot and I see Ivan bringing me a cricket, I see Josipina and Giacomino slapping her. With strong slaps. Josipina is bleeding. Karlo comes, he's holding a bit of the moon under his arm, and he says: Ballerina, you are silly. Then I look, I hear ships on the sea. I see ships, I see the sea, I see Elizabeta. Elizabeta is swimming and laughing. She's swimming toward me, then she stops. I see Mama helping her out of the sea and then the sea disappears and I don't see anything. I look back and see Greta Garbo. She isn't wearing anything. She's like me when my mama washes me. I know, I see myself in the little mirror in the hall. Greta Garbo comes closer and steps in front of me. She hugs me and I'm gone. Greta Garbo looks around and says: Ballerinaaaaa. Then I see the house, our yard, the village, the tree top and the field.

And I'm awake. Mama is looking down at me. I see her eyes. It's a new day. And I know that I have wet myself.

I'm in the kitchen now. My hair is combed. I'm standing in the corner, looking at the door. Mama is washing the handkerchiefs that *Tata* spit in. She'll put them out to dry in the yard. Then the postman comes. I don't want to see him. He always says something that makes me scared afterward and I stand on tiptoe and sing and throw whatever I find at the door. No use. I hear him. I hear his footsteps. He comes in. From the hall into the kitchen. With his cap on his head, his bag and his shoes that are heavy.

Ivanka, we're going to the moon! he says.

When? says Mama.

Next month. It says so in the newspaper. Sputnik is ready.

Is it?

Yes. It says it's been pointed right at the moon.

How?

I don't know. It's directed so that it'll go to the moon. They'll show it on television.

Will they?

Yes. Don't you have a television?

No.

But they'll still go to the moon, you know!

Oh, I know, I know, says Mama and pours him a drink.

He'll open his mouth. Mama and I will watch him. Then he'll close his mouth and laugh and then he'll leave and say something in the doorway. He does say something. Now.

Well, Ivanka, if you don't have a television, you can come to my house. I've put an aerial on the roof. You need an aerial, you get a better picture. The moon is far away!

Mama nods. The postman is leaving. I see him. He's crossing the yard. Mama says he hasn't brought any post, just told us that Sputnik is going to the moon. I don't know what Sputnik is. I think it must resemble Gina Lollobrigida, because she can fly, and I think Sputnik will fall and then there will be big holes in the earth, in our house, in the kitchen, it'll blow Mama from the earth. I stand on tiptoe. I stand on tiptoe, looking through the window. I see Mama hanging the handkerchiefs on the line. Then my toes hurt. I sing. I hear Mama, she's also singing in the yard. Then she comes closer, I hear that she's in the hall, I see her. She's standing in the door, laughing and singing. She's beautiful. She says she's old. She always says that she's old and she'll have to go to heaven when the time comes and that I'll go to heaven, too, because Ballerinas like me, Mama says, don't live very long after their Mama dies. I watch her sing. I listen to her. I stand on tiptoe and sing with Mama.

Vooolare, o, o . . . Cantare, o, o, o, o . . .

Suddenly Mama isn't singing anymore. She walks into the kitchen and starts setting the table. She says it's lunchtime, *Tata* will come, Karlo will come and Josipina will come for lunch, too. I don't want them to come for lunch. Let *Tata* stay in the bar, let Karlo stay in the woods, let Josipina do her ironing in secret. I grab a plate and throw it at the door. It breaks.

Ballerina! Mama says, picking up the plate. Then she goes to the pantry and gets the drops.

We're at the table now. Josipina, too. I've had the drops, I know, because I can only just hear her when she talks.

I read they're going to the moon, she says.

Not that soon, says Karlo.

On the twenty first of June! says *Tata*, slurping his minestrone.

So soon?! says Karlo.

I've bought a television, but Giacomino doesn't like it, says Josipina.

Why not? says *Tata*.

He says I'm silly now, if we have a television, I'll be even sillier.

Giacomino doesn't understand, says *Tata*. We'll buy a television, it's called Telefunken. You'll come and watch our television.

Who will buy a television? asks Karlo.

I will, says *Tata*, and goes on slurping his minestrone.

I see Mama smile. I hear her talk. Quietly. Mama is afraid that *Tata* will get angry, that's why she's talking quietly. Always. Mama says that we should instead buy paint to paint the house and make it healthier and whiter. I'm slurping my minestrone. I can't hear what they're saying anymore. *Tata* gets up. Now he's in the hall. He's coughing. Josipina is washing up. I hear something again. Josipina says that she will wash the dishes and then go. That she still has some ironing to do at the watchmaker's. Then she says the choir will sing at the celebration, there will be lots of people, there will even be recitations by actors. She says she can't remember when, that she has written it on a bit of paper. She says she's seen photos in the newspaper, that the great hall is full of chandeliers and stairs. She says it's in Trieste, not the village. Then I see her leave. Karlo is in the yard. They say hello. Karlo stays in the yard. He eats his minestrone under the chestnut tree. Karlo always eats his lunch twice. Mama says that Karlo, my brother, is strong, that he has to be strong because he walks around the woods and it's cold in the woods and there are animals.

Then *Tata* returns to the kitchen. I watch him. He turns on the lights on the gondola, switches on the Grundig and listens to the weather. Now he's sitting. I'm holding his ear and he's looking at the gondola with the lights.

Mama says they're going to the moon today and that days are passing terribly fast. She said this in the morning, when she was combing my hair in the hall. I'm sitting. *Tata* is with me. I'm holding his ear and he's watching the television that is called Telefunken. Karlo is in the kitchen, too. He's looking at the television. Mama is standing behind me. I can feel her hand on my shoulder.

Then a few more people come. I've never seen them before. I don't know them. They're looking at the television. Mama will tell me in the evening that these people don't have a television, that's why they were in our house and that they have painted houses and their houses are nice and healthy. I'm looking at the television, too.

There, says *Tata*. Now it'll land on the moon. We're all looking at the television. I see the box, I see something moving in it, someone talking. Someone I can't see. I listen. Someone says that Tito Stagno is a good commentator. I don't know who Tito Stagno is. I think that perhaps Uncle Feliks, who is already in heaven, knows about him. Then something moves in the television again and I see people wave. Someone says they're flags, American flags. We've landed on the moon! says *Tata* and turns off the television and turns on the lights on the gondola. Now I see a black box. Then I see that the people I don't know are leaving and that *Tata* and Karlo are in the yard. Mama is in the door. They're looking at the moon. You can only just see it, says Karlo, because it's still light.

And then *Tata* asks, do you think we're alone or is there another world? Oh, says Karlo, we're not alone, we're not alone. There are so many stars in the sky, when it's night, there must be some other people up there, surely!

I see Mama smile, lean on the door, she looks at me and then she says: And you, Ballerina, what do you think?

8

THE POSTMAN says there is no good in the world since they went to the moon years ago with Sputnik. He says the stars will take revenge and that things will be worse and worse in the world. As he says this, he puts a telegram on the table. I'm standing in the kitchen, looking at him. *Tata* is standing, too, looking through the window toward the yard as if he can't see the postman. The postman is standing in the door, looking at the telegram he's put on the table. Mama is looking at it, too. I'm looking at the postman. Mama doesn't get a glass, she doesn't pour him a drink. I'm standing in the corner, watching. I'm wearing a gray shirt and a blue skirt. Mama says that I got the skirt for my twenty-fifth birthday, Mama says I'm thirty now and that time goes quickly. She tells me this when she dresses me, after she has washed me and combed my hair in the hall in front of the mirror. I see everyone is looking at the telegram on the table. The postman said so. I've brought a telegram from Australia, he said and put it on the table. And then he talked about the moon and how there will be no good in the world. *Tata* is still looking through the window. He's smoking now, too, and shaking the ash onto the floor. Then Mama sweeps. Always, when *Tata* shakes the ash on the floor. I think *Tata* is looking at the sky, I think that he is quietly talking to Uncle Feliks, like Karlo. I think he wants to go to Uncle Feliks. The postman is still in the doorway. Then Mama picks up the telegram and says:

Here, Franc!

Tata takes the telegram and opens it. He looks at the postman and opens it. The postman is still standing in the door. Then *Tata* says:

Albert is coming, next week.

Mama's eyes light up. I see.

Is he coming with his wife? asks the postman.

Tata looks at him. *Tata* is looking at the postman in the doorway and doesn't say anything. Mama pours a glass. The postman drinks it, opens his mouth. We watch him. Mama sometimes says that she never knows if the postman will ever start breathing again after he has had a drink. Then he breathes. Always. He breathes, smiles and leaves.

Tata sits down. He looks at the gondola, sitting with the telegram in his hand. I'm still in the corner, looking at him.

I'm sitting at the table, eating pasta.

It's good, the pasta, isn't it, Ballerina? says *Tata*. I look at him. I know my mouth is full and the sauce is running down my chin. I know, I don't feel, because Mama gave me the drops earlier, to make me calm, I saw her. I know I don't feel. *Tata* is looking at his plate. Then I see there are others around the table, we're all here and I think it's my birthday. Josipina, Karlo, *Tata*, Mama, everybody is here. I look at them. Then I put down my fork with pasta on it and I hold his ear, Franc's, my father's. He doesn't say anything. He lets me pull his ear and he keeps looking at his plate with pasta. Then I take Karlo's hand and pinch him. First he moves it away, then lets me pinch him. I watch Josipina. Now I'm watching her and holding a fork. No one says anything. Not even Mama, who is standing behind me and eating pasta from a small pan. I see her. Mama likes pasta. Sometimes she says: Oooh, it's so good. And I watch Josipina. She looks like Mama. Her eyes are like Mama's, like Elizabeta's. Josipina, my sister.

She talks quietly. Mama says she talks like a sparrow, like the birds sleeping in the tree top when it's night. And sometimes when I lie and look from my bed at the window, with the chestnut tree outside, I think Josipina is up there with the birds sleeping in the tree.

And I watch her. She smiles and slowly picks up some pasta. Mama says Josipina is educated, that she's a teacher, but Giacomino said she should stay at home and look after the children. Poor Josipina, Mama says sometimes as we stand by the window, looking at the place where Mama had the best day in her life. The first day they were married, Giacomino hit her. Josipina cried, says Mama, because she was happy to have married Giacomino, but he didn't know she was crying because she was happy, and he hit her. Poor Josipina, says Mama, she's never cried since. And I watch her. I think I haven't seen her for a long time, only once when Karlo took me to her, because

Mama was tired and Elizabeta was ill. I know Karlo took me to her. I see her small apartment, I see Giacomino lying on the bed without clothes, reading a book. I hear Josipina tell me how he has read that book a few times already, then I hear her tell him to get dressed, then I see him get up from the bed and I see something dangling between his legs until he puts his pants on. Then I'm there, I know, in her kitchen and her children are with me, two boys. Mama says they're the same age as me, that they're my nephews and that they never come to visit. Mama says she's their *nona* and it would be nice if my nephews sometimes came for a visit.

Then I know I'm alone, that Giacomino who shoots at planes at night isn't there, that Josipina isn't there because she said she was going to iron a few things at the watchmaker's. And I'm alone with my two nephews. And I hear them say to me to come to their room and lie on the bed. I go to their room and I lie on the bed and my nephews lie next to me and they caress me. I know, they are caressing me on my face and then they caress my arms and then legs and I know my ears are ringing, that I'd like to say something, that I'd like to tell them something and I'd like to stand on tiptoe and sing and I'd like to hear Mama sing with me, and I'd like to be with Ivan, who is somewhere far away and going to school so that he can cure me, and I see the field, I suddenly see it full of weeds, I see my two nephews in the field, tramping it down and laughing and saying that there will never be any more potatoes in the field, that weeds will grow and that the field won't be able to breathe. And then I see rain falling on the field, on the weeds and on the nephews, who are laughing and saying that the weeds will grow even more because the sun will come out after the rain and it'll be warm and the weeds will grow even more, the weeds on the field, and then I sing, loud, loud . . .

Ciao, ciao, bambina! Un bacio ancor
e poi per sempre ti perderò …

And then I'm no longer at Josipina's. Then I'm home, like now in the kitchen and I'm just looking at her, at Josipina, picking up pasta with her fork.

Suddenly Mama says, Albert is coming from Australia.

He's coming with his *signorina*, says *Tata*, smiling. Mama says we must give him a good welcome, that he hasn't been home for twenty-five years and that we must forget everything. What happened, happened, says Mama and starts clearing the plates. I'm sitting at the table, listening. And Karlo says that he won't look at a whore in our house who went with the whole American barracks, that he doesn't give a shit if Albert fell in love with her.

I don't know what a whore is, I don't know what a whole American barracks is, I don't know what shit is and I don't know what it means that Albert fell in love with her. I feel warmth on my face, I'd like to get up and stand on tiptoe in the corner and look through the window at the yard.

Then *Tata* also says what happened, happened. Josipina's eyes are sparkling.

Mama says that Albert and Josipina loved each other very much and that she was very sad when he went to Australia. I watch Karlo. He drinks a glass of wine and looks at his plate.

After all, says *Tata*, if you have a job, it's because Albert went to Australia! Then Karlo lifts his eyes and also says: Well, what happened, happened. Now I want to get up, I want to push him into the yard, Karlo. Let him go to the woods, let him work, let him buy the paint so that we can paint the house. I feel Mama's hands on my shoulders. It's alright, it's alright, Ballerina. You'll see Albert and then it'll all be alright, she says. Then I stop thinking that I want to push Karlo into the yard and *Tata* says that the room needs to be prepared. That Albert and his *signorina* will sleep in the room Mama and he sleep in and that they will come to my room. We'll sleep with Ballerina, says *Tata* and looks at the gondola that always stands on the television that's called Telefunken. Then he says: Turn on the television, let's watch the news.

Josipina turns on the television and we watch the *telegiornale*.

Now it's evening. Mama and I are standing by the window and she says it's summer, the windows should stay open so that I can hear the crickets. Then she says: I'm really happy that Albert is coming, and she walks me to my bed. And then she leaves and closes the door. I lie there, listening to the crickets. I know I'm going to fall asleep soon.

Tata has gone to the barber's, says Mama, because Albert from Australia is coming today. She's combing my hair. She has dressed me in a pink dress with a bow, the one I wore for my birthday, once in the past. I know that that was then. Ivan was still here and said to me, Happy Birthday, Ballerina, and he gave me a bunch of flowers. I looked down at him because he was little and his ears stuck out.

Mama's hair is nicely combed, too, and she's wearing her party dress with the nice, starched collar. Karlo went to Venice airport with his car that isn't his. Mama said that Karlo is going to pick up Albert at the airport, when I stood at the window and everything was blue, even the yard was blue as I watched Karlo leave.

They'll be here any moment now, says Mama, looking through the window at the yard. I'm standing by the door, looking at her. She's looking through the window, walking up and down, up and down. Then she says: Josipina is here …

I see her. She's crossing the yard, coming into the hall, then the kitchen.

Srečko is coming, too, says Mama to Josipina.

Good, says Josipina, taking her shoes off. She says they're too tight because they're new. I look at her. She's sitting at the table, rubbing her toes.

Then Mama says Srečko is here, too. I don't know if it is him, I don't know if this is Srečko, my cousin, like Mama says, because his mama was Lucija, the sister of Franc, who is my *Tata*.

In the evening, as we are standing by the window before it is night, Mama says that she hasn't seen him for a long time, Srečko, only Karlo sometimes meets up with him and then comes home drunk, Mama says. She's looking at the field, at the cherry tree and she says: He must have aged, Srečko …

Mama says that when a person gets old like she has, they soon go to heaven.

I hope he doesn't get lost, says Mama then and puts me to bed.

Now Srečko is in the kitchen. Mama steps closer to him. I see her. She goes to him, puts her arms around him and then strokes his thin hair. He smiles. I see he has very few teeth. *Allora*, our Australian's coming, he says, nodding. Mama smiles. I see she's happy. When Mama is happy, I'm not scared. Everyone is happy because Albert is coming, even Josipina, even Karlo and *Tata*, who's still at the barber's.

Mama says that Albert and Srečko are very fond of each other. That they used to fish together in the pond, they rode bicycles together and wherever one went, the other followed.

How time passes, eh, Srečko, she says and looks through the window at the yard.

Now *Tata* is coming. We all see him through the window. He's in the yard. He stops. I see the back of his neck and the straw hat. You can see his hair has been cut, you see it under his hat, on the back of his neck. When *Tata's* hair has been cut, I feel as if I want to cry, I want to sob, because he looks like a little boy, like Ivan when he goes to school or when they cut his hair for the holidays. We must look nice on holidays, says Mama, and today is a holiday, and she goes out into the yard where *Tata* is.

We're all in the yard.

We're standing under the chestnut tree, in which birds sleep at night, looking at the gap where, Mama says, Karlo will bring Albert. It's nice in the shade, says Srečko, wiping his forehead. I see his hand, how it trembles. He wipes his forehead with a trembling hand and says: Oh, they should be back from Venice by now.

And we all look in the direction Karlo, Albert and his *signorina* should come. I don't know. I've never seen his *signorina*, she hasn't been in our kitchen yet so that I could see her.

Mama says she had long red hair, that she was very beautiful and that she's called Ida. She told me this once by the window as she looked toward Mount Čaven and Angel Mountain, which is hers and hers only, she says.

I hear a car. The others hear it too. I see. *Tata* takes a step forward, adjusts his hat, Mama adjusts her skirt, Josipina wipes the dust off her shoes and Srečko once more wipes his forehead. I see his eyes are sparkling, Srečko's.

The car is here. Albert, my brother steps out, Ida, his *signorina*, follows him. They both have a lot of dry leaves on their clothes because in the car driven by Karlo there's always a lot of dry leaves. I know this from when he drives me to Elizabeta's and he opens the window and the leaves twirl around me. Karlo says: It's draughty. I'll close the window.

Karlo is smiling. So are Albert and Ida. They walk toward us. They are coming closer. Now they are here. *Tata* hugs Albert. They hold on to each other firmly. *Tata* cries. Then he isn't crying any more. Then Albert goes to Mama and kisses her. He caresses her gray hair and her face and holds her hands. And then he kisses Josipina, hugs Srečko and me. Hello, Ballerina, he says. Ida is there, the *signorina*. I see her. She's standing at a distance, smiling. In the evening Mama will tell me that she was embarrassed, poor Ida. In the evening, when Mama sleeps in my room and *Tata* is in my room, too. Then I see Mama step over to Ida and shake her hand. *Tata* does the same, as do Josipina and Srečko.

Now we're in the kitchen. I'm looking at Albert, my brother from Australia. He has beautiful eyes, Albert, like the sea, says Mama. Ida has similar eyes. Mama says that people who love each other always have something in common on their faces.

Albert and Ida are handing out parcels. One for everyone. Mama says that they are presents and we must open them. I see *Tata* has already opened his. Mama says it's an ashtray in the shape of Australia. Oooh, how beautiful it is, she says. Then Karlo unwraps his present. Mama says he got a bottle with photographs of kangaroos. It's Josipina's turn. She unwraps it slowly. Then she says: Oooh, what a beautiful plate! and she shows us it. I see Josipina holding the plate. Then I hear Albert say that a photograph of the capital of Australia is stuck on the plate. Everyone says once more: Oooh, how nice it is. Then Srečko unwraps his present. Albert says that it's a barrel organ, where you have to turn the handle and then music plays. Albert says that it plays the song *Lili Marleen*. Then Mama says I should unwrap my present. I can't. She helps me. I see her hands untie the ribbon and remove the paper, then I see a box, I see Mama opening it and then everyone says: Oooh! Look how beautiful it is, says Mama and tells me I got a dancer, a ballerina, like me, only I don't have a short, lacy skirt, Mama says and turns something on the box the dancer is standing on, Ballerina, me. Then Ballerina twirls and moves her legs, up, down, up, down. Then Mama opens her present. And again everyone says: Oooh! What a beautiful headscarf, thank you, Albert, thank you, Ida, says Mama and puts the headscarf back in the paper. I'm standing in the corner now. Looking at them. Albert and Ida. And the others. They're drinking, eating and talking. Albert is talking about wooden houses. He says that he builds small wooden houses, that the deserts in Australia are big and there are many fires. Then he says he will stay a month, visit his friends, and then go back.

Then they go on drinking. I see Mama. She's looking at Albert's face and listening. I see she's happy and I'm not afraid of anything. I haven't had my drops and I'm not afraid. I'm holding Ballerina in my hands and listening. Srečko is talking now. He says he will go to Vienna, to visit Beethoven's grave, because Beethoven has been in heaven for a long time, Mama says. Then they pour wine for Srečko. Karlo pours it and Srečko is talking and talking and everyone is laughing and then Srečko sings some music written by Beethoven, he tells us, and then he cries and everyone keeps laughing, like they always do when Srečko is talking about Beethoven and crying and the others laugh. I look at Ida. She's looking at Mama. Mama doesn't see that Ida is looking at her, Mama is also laughing because everyone is laughing and if it's a holiday, she always says, everybody needs to be happy.

Then I see Karlo go to the pantry. I know he'll come back with the accordion. He's already here, sitting, pulling the bellows, as *Tata* says. And then Karlo plays and Albert dances with Mama and *Tata* dances with Ida and then I want to stand on tiptoe, look at the yard and sing. My ears are ringing, I'm standing on tiptoe, singing.

Ciao, ciao, bambinaaaaaa!
Un bacio ancooor …

Then Karlo is no longer playing the accordion. I see Mama quickly go to the pantry. I know she'll give me the drops. I pick up the plate that Josipina was given as a present and throw it at the door.

Oooh, everyone says and Mama comes back from the pantry and

gives me the drops.

I see Albert and Ida looking at me. Everyone is looking at me, then they smile and Mama picks up the bits of the plate with the capital of Australia on it. I'll glue it together, says Josipina and smiles. Then Srečko picks up the barrel organ and turns the handle so that the song *Lili Marleen* is played.

La la, la la la la, la la, la la la la …

And he sings quietly and turns the handle. Then he smiles and everyone claps.

9

MAMA SAYS Albert and Ida have been here for two weeks and that today we're going to a party so that Albert can see his friends and he and Ida can dance, that they're always at home and not going anywhere, that they keep looking through the window at the yard, walking by the field and that they haven't spoken to anyone for days.

Then I see Albert and Ida, at night, when I wake up I see them. Now I wake up every night and see them, Albert and Ida in Mama's room. I get off the bed, by myself. I think of Ivan who goes to school so that he can cure me and then I go in the room where Albert and Ida are sleeping and it's light, because Mama says the moon is in the sky, that they went up there with the Sputnik and things are bad in the world since we landed on the moon. Then I stand in front of the door to the room where Albert and Ida are sleeping, the door is ajar and the light is shining on their bed. I watch and listen. I see Albert and Ida, they're holding each other and aren't wearing any clothes and are kissing on the mouth and caressing each other, and then I hear. Albert says something first and Ida answers.

Are you happy?

Yes.

You're not sorry we came?

No. Let me kiss you.

I can't, I can't tonight, Ida.

OK.

Sorry, but I feel as if, as if …

It's alright, Albert, it's alright … Come here, go to sleep, go to sleep …

She says this every night. Come here Albert, go to sleep, go to sleep … And then I watch them. I think they have similar eyes and if two people love each other, Mama says, they always have some similarities in their faces. Then I think that Mama and Aunt Elizabeta also love each other because they are the same, and I go to my bed. *Tata* is snoring. I know Mama is happy when *Tata* snores, because it's like when they told her, wait, come again, Franc will come, you'll see how handsome he is. And he came, Franc, and he was handsome and they married and he snored. Franc, my *Tata*.

Now we're at the party, Mama says, and she looks at Albert and Ida. Karlo is with us, too. I know Mama is going to buy me Coca Cola, when we go to a party. I've always known this. I like the bubbles and then I belch and Mama says: Not so loud!

Karlo says the band will play now, we should sit down, have a drink and then there will be dancing. I know what I'll drink. I'll drink Coca Cola and belch.

We're sitting at a table. Karlo says it's a farmers' holiday, that there are tractors if we want to look at them. I know what tractors are. Mama says I've always wanted to go on a tractor since when I was little and still talking. She says I sat on the tractor and wanted it to move and she and *Tata* had to shake the tractor so that it seemed as if it was moving, and I shouted, Go! Go! Mama says in the evening when we are standing by the window and looking at the chestnut tree, at the yard, the field, the cherry tree and her Angel Mountain next to Mount Čaven, already far off in the dark.

We're sitting at the table. Karlo is putting the drinks on the table. The Coca Cola is for me, Mama pours it. The band is playing. Karlo says they're from the next village and that they're good and that they also play at funerals when anyone dies.

Albert and Ida are looking straight ahead. They're smiling. Albert says he doesn't recognize anyone and asks Karlo where everyone he used to know has gone. Karlo says he doesn't know, that he spends most of his time in the woods and doesn't know.

Mama asks Ida if she has a job in Australia, Mama says she hasn't asked her yet even though she's been meaning to and that Ida should forgive her for not asking. Ida says that she works as a maid for a family. I know what a maid is and I know I'm drinking Coca Cola with bubbles and belching.

Sshh, quieter, Ballerina, says Mama.

Then Karlo says he's going to get some chicken. He's going there, he says, they're roasting chickens, and the band is still playing. I'm watching them. Then I look at Albert and Ida, they're looking around, smiling, and they say nothing. Mama is looking at the band and also smiling. I go on drinking Coca Cola with bubbles.

Then we eat chicken. Karlo says it's good. Albert nods and Ida smiles. Ida says she doesn't eat chicken. I look at Mama. Mama is wearing her headscarf from Australia over her shoulders, a headscarf with flowers. She's eating chicken with a headscarf on her shoulders and her face is flushed. Oh, how embarrassed I am, she says sometimes and then becomes red. Like now.

The band is no longer playing. Karlo says that now another group is playing for people to dance. He says he doesn't dance. Albert smiles and asks him when he will get married. Mama says she would be very happy if Karlo did get married, fixed that hole of his in the attic and bought some paint and painted the house white. Karlo says nothing. I go on drinking Coca Cola. Karlo has brought me another one. And I watch. People are dancing, Mama says why don't you two go and dance and she looks at Albert. Albert smiles, so does Ida. Then I go back to watching people dance, they twirl and I get dizzy. Someone comes to our table, looking at me. Everyone is looking at me. I don't want to be looked at, not by everyone, not by someone. I want to get up, I want to stand on tiptoe, I want to sing. Mama takes my hand. Sit, she says, this is Albert's friend. I sit. I see Albert leave with his friend. They hug and talk. Then I see Ida. She's sitting and looking at the people dancing in front of her. Then she gets up and leaves. Mama looks after her. She smiles. I want to stand up. I want to pee, a lot, for all the days and all the mornings. I think I could pee so much that everyone would drown and Mama and Karlo and Ida and Albert would climb on a tree and watch people dancing under water. They always dance, I know.

I get up, I stand on tiptoe. Mama doesn't say anything. Karlo has also gone somewhere. I see clouds, they're moving quickly. Mama says they're coming from the sea, that it will rain. There's thunder. I sing. Mama says: You can sing, no one can hear you because there's music and dancing. I sing and look at the clouds. I want to go after them, I step forward and then stand on tiptoe again, I sing and look at the clouds, they're moving. Then I feel a drop on my face. Mama says it's raining. I feel the wind. I see clouds running away even faster and feel more and more rain on my face. I sing. People are running, covering themselves. I sing and when I don't sing, when I feel like picking up something and throwing it at the door, I belch. There's no door here, no kitchen, no yard, no chestnut tree with the birds. Mama takes me by the arm and says we must get under cover so that we don't get wet. We walk to where they're roasting chickens. I see them. There are lots of them, chickens. There's a little roof, says Mama.

We're standing under the little roof where they're roasting chickens. It is thundering and raining. Mama is wondering where Karlo, Ida and Albert are.

Don't be afraid, Ballerina, she says then. They'll come.

10

MAMA SAYS IT's winter and the door must be closed. She says this as we stand by the window, looking at the yard. Then she says she doesn't know if she will ever see Albert again. He left just like that, she says. He said, Ida and I are going back! All of a sudden he said this, without even looking at her. Then, she says, they packed their suitcases without talking and she was standing in the door watching them pack. Then she told them, wait a little longer, don't go so soon. And then, says Mama, they said their goodbyes in the yard and Ida smiled at her and Albert kissed her and *Tata* asked Albert what it's like on an airplane, because he had never been in one. And Albert told them about the plane, about the clouds on which ice gathers on the side away from the sun, and that the ice moves from one cloud to another, not just ice but also hail, snow, rain. That everything rolls and moves. That it's nice when the sun is setting and the plane is flying over the sea, that it's nice when on one side you see the day and on the other side the night and you're flying toward the day and toward the night and there is a storm and you see lightning and the plane shakes and you're scared. Mama says that *Tata* was listening with his mouth open and it seemed, says Mama, as if *Tata* was getting ready to go up into the clouds, the ice, the snow, the day and the night. Then they got into the car, says Mama, and Karlo took them to Venice airport. Albert said he would write, says Mama. Maybe now, for the holidays, she says and walks me to my bed. Good night, Ballerina, she says and her voice is quiet and I think I can hear Josipina, who is sleeping with the birds in the tree and is like a sparrow.

Now it's a new day. Mama says it's still winter. I know it is because I'm wearing stockings, because Mama put them on me in the morning. I'm in the kitchen, in the corner, watching Mama, watching her hands pick up a log and put it in the stove, and she closes her eyes because, she says, the flame is so big and hot. Oooh, how it burns, says Mama. *Tata* is in the hall. He's combing his hair, looking at himself in the mirror and combing. Karlo is working, says Mama, Karlo is in the woods, guarding the trees and guarding the animals and making sure the animals have food because it's cold, says Mama, and it may start snowing and then the animals have nothing to eat. *Tata* walks into the kitchen. I see him. He's coming into the kitchen through the door. He walks to the window, looks at the thermometer. He says it's zero. Then he takes a pencil off the fridge and writes on the calendar that it is zero and cloudy. Mama says he always writes in the calendar whether it is sunny, cloudy or rainy. He writes it down, says Mama. And then he goes to the bar. Every day. Now he says, I'm going to the bar, and puts his hat on. I see him, he's in the hall now, opening the main door, now he's in the yard. I see him, he's in the yard. He's looking at the leafless chestnut tree, then he looks at the kitchen, I see him, he's looking at me. He lifts his hat, looks at me, smiles, puts the hat back on, and walks off. To the bar. I know, because *Tata* said: I'm going to the bar. Then I don't see him any more. All I see is the window and through it a bit of the yard, the trunk of the chestnut tree, the thermometer with the zero and a slice of the sky. That's what I see, I know.

Then I leaf through the magazine and Mama is standing behind me, talking to me and pointing at people with her finger. She says that these are people on photographs, they're not real, and then I think that the people I see leafing through the magazine as Mama stands behind me, I think these people are in heaven like Aunt Lucija, like Uncle Feliks, and I think Uncle Feliks has lots of friends.

Then Mama laughs. She points at a man, says it is Charlie, that the man cutting a shoe on a plate with a knife and a fork is called Charlie Chaplin. And she says we can watch him on television on Saturdays after lunch and we laugh, I also laugh when I watch him, Karlo laughs and *Tata* laughs.

Then Mama says it's lunchtime. Karlo is sitting at the table. I see him, I run into him and I want him to go back to the woods, to go and work, to buy the paint so that we can paint the house white. Karlo is holding my hands, saying, be good, Ballerina, be good! I push him even more and Karlo is in the yard. I see him. And suddenly I see another man. Karlo is no longer alone. There's a man with him who hasn't been in our kitchen yet. The man is saying something. Karlo nods, then I see he leaves the man alone in the yard and suddenly I see Karlo in the kitchen again. I'm going to the bar, he says, *Tata* isn't feeling too well. And I see Mama looking after him, I see her bun of gray hair, her shoulders. Mama is looking at the yard and I'm looking at her, at her bun of gray hair.

It's evening now and Mama and I are standing by the window. Mama says nothing can be seen because in the winter night falls earlier and then you can't see anything. Mama says everything is black, but the chestnut tree is still there, the yard is still there, the hills are in the distance, the valley is there and Angel Mountain is still there. And then she says that *Tata* has gone to heaven. Mama is talking quietly again. Like Josipina in the tree top. Mama says we won't see him anymore, that Karlo was too late, that *Tata* was already covered with a white sheet. That he just stayed sitting at the table with cards in his hand, that he was then covered with a white sheet and that we won't see him again, Franc, who was handsome and came and I married him, says Mama.

Then I think I'm in the kitchen and I see the window, I see the thermometer, I see the tree trunk, I see the yard and the slice of the sky and I don't see Franc, who is my *Tata*. I don't see Franc, who looks through the window, takes his hat off and smiles at me. I want to hold his ear, I want to squeeze his ear so that he bends toward me and says: It's alright, Ballerina, it's alright!

I want him to light the lights on the gondola and I want him to say: We must buy a television, you can see the whole world on it.

Then I look at Mama and I think that I can see a slice of the sky through the window and I think that's where heaven is, that *Tata* is happy if he's there with Uncle Feliks and Aunt Lucija. Then Mama says something. I listen to her. Tomorrow there will be snow!

Mama and I are standing by the window again. Mama says the funeral was today and *Tata* is now in heaven for ever. She's holding my hand and tells me, like she used to, that we all go to heaven, that she will go there one day and so will I. Then I see her hand, it's lifting, I see it, it's lifting by the window, in front of the darkness, because it's winter outside, and then Mama says: You see, Ballerina, it hurts here, where my heart is, this is where it hurts. And I see her hand rest on her chest. Mama says that's the chest and that's where we have a heart. And suddenly she says:

Someone has put on the light in the yard. It's Karlo!

And she leans to the window and says:

Look, Ballerina, it's snowing, tomorrow everything will be white. Our house will be white, too.

And we look through the window. Mama says there are snow-flakes and there are lots of them, they're white and they come from the sky.

I'm looking at the snowflakes and thinking that *Tata* has come to say hello, all white and in small bits, that our house will be all white, like Mama says. It'll be all white and then I think Karlo has bought the paint and he'll paint the door as well and we'll have a white door.

Then Mama and I stand by the window, looking at the sky, snowflakes falling from it, and I think that our house is moving, that it has left the earth and we are flying into the air. Mama, me, and the house.

And Karlo, my brother. That we're flying like Albert, like Ida into the sky.

11

I WATCH HER, my mama. I watch her in the kitchen. She says I'm ready, I'm washed and dressed and that we're going to have our photographs taken to get a picture for the border pass, she only has to comb her hair. I see her, she's in the hall, combing her long, gray hair. I see her through the kitchen door, because it is open. I'm afraid because Mama is combing her hair. I watch her hands in her hair, I'm scared they'll get tangled up and stay there, her hands. She's looking at herself in the little mirror and combing her hair. She says it's alright that *Tata* went to heaven, now she and I will go to Ajdovščina, Karlo will take us, as soon as we have the pass. Mama says that the car broke down when it was *Tata's* funeral. There he was, covered in flowers in the car, and when they drove past the bar, it stopped and had to be pushed to the cemetery. From the bar, says Mama, which was *Tata's* real home and where he had died and where they covered him with a sheet, to the cemetery. Mama says there was no choir and no band at the funeral, that the priest said *Tata* should rest in peace, sprinkled him and told him to rest in peace. She's saying this as she combs her hair, arranging it in a bun, and then I see her neck, thin, thin, and then she says we're going to get some bread and going to the photographer's, so that he can take a picture for the pass and then we can go to Ajdovščina. And she fastens her hair and looks back at me. She says that she hasn't been to Ajdovščina for twenty-five years, that it is a very long time and that time goes very quickly.

Then we're on the road, like before, I know. First the yard, then the path, then the gap in the hedge and then the road and the bend and the church and another road and then there are shops. Mama says: When you were little, you always went with me, every morning, to get bread and milk. At one time we didn't buy milk, she says, then Greta was in the stable and she gave us fine milk.

We walk along the road, past the church. Slowly, because Mama says that my toes are hurting and that she will put some cream on them in the evening. Mama says Nivea is the best cream. And then I see people on the road. They're looking at me. Mama says that they're looking at me because I'm beautiful, because we're going to the photographer's, we're both beautiful. I see Mama. She's holding my hand and walking slowly. Mama is wearing the dress with a starched collar. This dress is always nice, she says. If you starch the collar, it's always nice, she says. I look at the people. Sometimes they smile and nod and walk on by. Mama also smiles, nods, squeezes my hand and pulls me on.

Then we stand. We're going to get bread, she says, and we go in. I see cupboards with drawers, I see candy, I see Coca Cola, I see bread. Mama says: A small loaf, and then I see a woman take a loaf and hide it in paper, then I see her smile and look at me. She comes closer and presses some candy into my hand. Oh, thank you, Armida, says Mama, picks up the bag with the loaf in, takes my hand and we go through the door onto the road. Mama says that this shop is always empty, that we have bought a small loaf and that it will be enough for today because Karlo isn't coming for lunch. That he has taken a *prosciutto* and cheese *panino* with a bit of wine, that he will be full and won't be thirsty. Here, she says then, come, this is it. And then we stand in front of the door first and Mama is looking at some displays and says that there are photographs in there, that they were young, the people in them, when they got married, the grooms and brides in those display cases. *Tata* and I were also a bride and groom, she says, but not now, she says, when we were young. Then she says they got married, her and *Tata*. That it was early morning and the sexton came to be their witness because he got up early because he had to ring the Ave Maria and was always there in the church, even early in the morning and even when Mama and *Tata* got married, and that they also went to a fair, she says, after they were married, they took the train and went to a fair in Gorizia and in the evening they were home and he snored. Oh, I was so happy; and she pulls me inside.

We're at the photographer's now, says Mama. She says we must wait because there are lots of people. We stand and wait. He's inside, in that room there, says Mama. We'll go in there, she says, that's where the pictures are made. Now it's our turn, she says. I see two girls. Mama says that they must have been to communion because they're wearing white. The girls look at me. They're as small as Ivan. I think about him. I see him. He comes through the door into the kitchen and says: Happy Birthday, Ballerina, and I look down at him because he is small and his ears stick out. Then the girls leave and a lady goes after them. I look at her. She's fat, the lady, and the girls are thin. She speaks. You stupid girl, says the lady, you must smile next time, you stupid thing, she says, and hits the girl on the head, pushing her out and going out after her. Then the man comes and looks at Mama. And she says: We'd like to have a photo taken for a pass. And we go into the little room.

Now I'm sitting. Mama says that there's blue material behind me so that I can look beautiful, so that it seems like there's the sea behind me. I sit and look. He comes over to me, takes my face in his hand, says I have to look at that box, that he'll say to me, look at the little birdie, and I will have to smile. Mama is there, on the other side of the box, looking at me and smiling. I can feel my toes, they're hurting. I want to be home, in the kitchen, looking at the yard. Then Mama says: Be good, Ballerina, it'll be quick, it doesn't hurt, you'll see a light. And then he's by the box, hiding behind the box, and he says: Look at the birdie, look at the birdie. Mama also says: Look at the birdie, oooh, how pretty it is. I can't see a bird, it's asleep in that tree top in the yard, when it's night, it sleeps and Josipina sleeps with it in the tree. I see her. Mama says Josipina is like a bird and I see her there in the chestnut tree, among the leaves. And then I see the light and Mama says: There, you see, it didn't hurt … Then he comes over to me. I see his mouth, his head. Shame you didn't smile, he says and strokes my face and I want to bite his finger, his hand, his face and then I want to be in the kitchen, looking at the yard.

Now wait here, says Mama, sitting me on a chair. Now I'm not in the little room any more. Mama says she won't be long, that I should sit, that she'll come back soon, and I'm afraid that she'll be in pain and that she'll be scared by the light, and then I want to sing, stand on tiptoe, look at the yard and sing. Then I hear Mama talking. She says when we get the pass, we're going to where she came from, Karlo will take us to Ajdovščina, if there's time we'll go and see where the *burja* wind is born. She says that it is born in her village, which is in a beautiful valley and that one part of the valley is so beautiful, so very beautiful that you can't imagine it, she says. That the wind blows and the trees grow at an angle in her valley. She says we'll cross the border with the pass, and go to her valley, in which there's also a river, green and blue and straight, and when there's a lot of rain, the river floods the fields. And above all this, above the valley, above the slanting trees, above the river and the rain, there's her mountain, Angel Mountain, says Mama, where she and Elizabeta went before they came to Trieste and where she found it infinitely beautiful. Mama says it means a lot if you find one beautiful day in your life and you remember it for the rest of your life. And she goes on talking and then he says: *Un momento, signora.* He comes out of the little room, looks at me, goes to another room and Mama goes on talking. I hear her. I know she's there, sitting like I sat, in front of the sea, I know her collar is starched and she's beautiful because we'll get the pass. Mama says that Angel Mountain is as beautiful as our field when it's covered in snow and everything is so quiet and soft. Then I see him again. He looks at me, smiles and goes to the room where Mama is. Now Mama isn't talking any more. I know she'll look at the little bird, smile and then she'll see a light, in that little room.

Now it's evening and Mama and I are standing by the window. Mama says the pictures will be ready in a few days, then Karlo will go to the police and sort out all the documents for our passes. We're looking out of the window and Mama is talking. She says that there are three of us in the house: me, Karlo and her. That Karlo could get married, he could have children and then the house would be alive and healthy, like all houses where children can be heard crying and laughing. Then she talks about Josipina, she says that Josipina is a hard-working wife and if Karlo doesn't get married, she'll look after him, washing and ironing for him. She won't have to cook, Karlo is a good cook.

I'm looking through the window, at the yard. Mama says the moon is in the sky, that's why we can't see the stars so well. Then I think of the birds, the yard, the hills, the field and the cherry tree, and then the hills again and the valley that is Mama's. Then Mama walks me to the bed. You'll see how nice it will be, she says, Karlo will take us, when we get our passes, and she strokes me. I see her. I see her eyes, her hands. Then she moves away, I see her. She stops in the door, looks at me once more and says: Good night, Ballerina, and she closes the door a little, leaving it ajar.

12

KARLO IS IN the yard. Mama says he's probably cold, that it's the fall, that I shouldn't push him into the yard. I see him. He's sitting on a chair under the chestnut tree. I saw him take the chair from the kitchen and slide it to the yard. He's sitting on it, eating an apple. My mama gave me the drops earlier. You'll see, it'll all be alright. Now, as always, I don't feel anything. Mama says the drops are a medicine so that she doesn't get too tired, so that I don't have to go to Elizabeta's and that they never come and take me away in a car. Then she goes in the yard, I see her, Karlo is talking to her. Mama is listening. I see him. He's saying something to her, then Mama looks at the chestnut tree and Karlo walks toward the house. I see him. He's already in the hall, he walks into the kitchen. He doesn't look at me. Then Mama comes. She's looking at Karlo, saying:

And who told you this?

In the inn, they telephoned the inn, says Karlo.

And now?

And now nothing. That's how it is. He left and they can't find him. It's been a month and he hasn't come back. He took a bag, came to the inn, drank half a liter of wine and said he was going to the station, and that's that. He's gone, *basta*, vamoose, disappeared into thin air, nothing you can do, *fanculo porca puttana*, I told him he'd get lost, *testa di cazzo*. He should've stayed at home and listen to Beethoven, but no, *puttana eva*. Why did he have to fuck off to Vienna when he wasn't even capable of just getting some bread, when he hasn't done anything in his life, and then he goes to Vienna. And he got there. They phoned from the hotel. He left everything in his room, his bag, his pants, his jacket, but he was gone. They found the number in his pants, the phone number of the inn, and they called, from the hotel. They said he was gone, they had called the police, but he was gone. What's the point of calling the police, *puttana eva*, when he's a moron. In his underpants, not even aware that he's naked and God knows where he got lost. Bloody hell, I told him to stay at home, to listen to music on the record player. You can't go somewhere at his age. I sleepwalk, but I do it on the field, among the potatoes, I don't go to fucking Vienna. *Ecco*, and now he's gone.

He isn't talking any more, Karlo. He's sitting, pouring a glass and drinking. Poor Srečko, says Mama, looking at the yard. Then Karlo lifts his eyes. I see his eyes are bright. I think he's crying. My eyes are bright, when I cry. Then he says:

He's a moron, not poor.

And then we don't talk.

It's evening now. I'm in the kitchen. I'm sitting looking at a picture of Greta Garbo. Mama is behind me, her hands on my shoulders, she's looking at the pictures with me and I know she'll say: Oooh, *mamma mia*, look how beautiful she is. And then I see her tidying up, turning on the lights on the gondola, dusting the television so that she can turn it on and watch it. Then I see her laughing, watching the television, I see her laughing and she says I should watch, I should listen, so that I can also laugh, that these televisions are good. Then I watch. I see two men. Mama says they're men because they wear trousers, not dresses. Not with butterflies or a bow. Then Mama says those two men are Laurel and Hardy, but she never knows which one is Laurel and which Hardy, whether Hardy is the thin one and Laurel the fat one or the other way round. And she laughs. And I watch Laurel and Hardy. They're on a plane. Mama says they're on a plane and that the plane is broken and they're coming up with all sorts of ideas so as not to crash. And then I see the plane crash. The thin one is alive, he gets up from the mud the plane has crashed into and he looks for the fat one, and then he sees him. He sees that the fat one has wings and a hat and says goodbye to him as he flies up to heaven.

Then Karlo comes. I see him. He's already sitting in the kitchen, saying that he'll watch the weather on the Ljubljana channel, that they always get the weather right there. He's sitting and looking at the television and I hear them say that it will rain, but I don't know where or when. Then I know Karlo will fall asleep on the chair and Mama will say: Come, Ballerina, we'll brush our teeth and then we'll go to bed, for tomorrow is a new day. And I know I'll wet myself and then it will be a new day, it will be morning and Mama will wash me and it will be like it used to be. And if I don't dream, I'll throw everything out of the window, and if I don't throw everything out of the window, I'll simply get up and think of Ivan, who will cure me, and then I'll open the door and will look at Mama sleeping and I'll see she's alone because *Tata* is already in heaven.

Mama is holding my hand, we're walking through the kitchen door, Karlo is behind us, on the chair, asleep. Then we go to the hall, where the following day I'll look at myself in the mirror, then we walk upstairs and come to my room and Mama changes me and then we stand by the window, where it's dark.

Mama says that everything is so strange today. Poor Srečko, she says, he's sure to have got lost there, in Vienna. How strange, she says. Josipina said she would come by today, but she didn't, how strange, she says. Karlo should have brought our passes today, so that we can go to Ajdovščina, she says, but I forgot to ask him if they were ready. How strange, she says, I dreamt about Albert and Ida and Franc last night, she says. I'll play the lottery, she says, we'll get lots of money and we'll fix the house and Karlo will get some paint and everything will be right. I'll play the lottery, she says. And she looks at me. Now we're looking at each other and Mama doesn't say anything. She takes my hand, walks me to my bed and she doesn't say: Good night, Ballerina. She doesn't say anything. She doesn't stroke me and she doesn't push the door to.

I see her go through the door and she doesn't close it or push it to, nothing, and it's night and I look at the darkness on the roof and I remember the dream that I'm flying, catching the clouds, that I'm falling, that I see the house with the roof, with stones on it, that I see the yard with the chestnut tree, that I'm afraid I'll wake up the birds sleeping in the tree. And then I know I'm going to wet myself and then I know it will be a new day, like now.

I see. The room is as blue as Mama when she comes into the room. There's no Mama. I lie and wait. I don't hear footsteps. I know I have wet myself, that Mama will wash me and that I'll be in the kitchen and I'll stand on tiptoe and I'll sing and Mama will sing with me. Mama sings nicely and she sings better than the choir and talks more nicely than the others out there, on the road, from the gap in the hedge to the left, near the church, in the cultural centre.

I listen. No Mama. I feel cold. I get up. I think of Ivan, who will cure me, and then I go. I'm moving, I know. I'm approaching the door. I see it, it's getting closer. It's open. I walk through the door, I come to Mama's room. The door is open. I push it. Mama is on the carpet by the bed. I walk closer. Now I'm next to her. I look at her. Mama is lying on the carpet, not moving. I watch her. I think she has also dreamt about the clouds, that she is flying, falling. Mama's eyes are open, as blue as the morning. Then I take her hand. I lean over first and take her hand. I want her to stand up, I want her to come to my room and say: Good morning, Ballerina. I'm holding her hand, pulling her toward me. Mama and the carpet come with me. I'm turning her around me, I want her to get up. Then I think Mama is laughing, that it's tickling her, and I laugh and sit down next to her on the carpet and look her in the eyes that are blue, and I think I see her in the kitchen door. I'm standing on tiptoe in the kitchen, looking at the door. I see Mama talking to someone and she says that sometimes it happens to children that they stop talking and playing, that they hear everything, but they no longer talk, that with time it gets worse. And then I see her look at me and say: What will come of us, Ballerina? And then I see her here, now, on the carpet, with her eyes open, with long gray hair, which she will later put in a bun in the hall, and I'll see her neck, her thin, thin neck, and then we'll be in the hall and we'll sing, holding hands, we'll sing:

Vooolare, o, o!

Cantareee, o, o, o, o!

And then I'll drink Coca Cola and I will belch and Mama will say: Not so loud, and then I'll throw plates at the door, I'll throw them so hard that they'll break into thousands of pieces and Mama will pick them up, and then I'll look at Greta Garbo and Gina Lollobrigida and Laurel and Hardy and then we'll sing again, Mama and I, when she wakes up, we'll sing:

Ciao, ciao, bambina, un bacio ancor …

13

KARLO SAYS MAMA has been in heaven for a long time. He always tells me that when I stand in front of her room and look at the door and stand on tiptoe because I think I'll see her then, Mama, who has been in heaven for a long time. Then I want to hear what she's talking about to Uncle Feliks, Aunt Lucija and to Franc, who is my *Tata*. And then Karlo says:

Stop looking at that door, come down, Ballerina, I'll make you some coffee and give you biscuits.

Then I go. I follow Karlo, down the stairs, to the hall, to the kitchen. I look at his broad shoulders, his checked shirt, his pants. Mama says that Karlo's pants are always stained with tree sap because tree sap doesn't come off.

Then I eat biscuits, brought by Josipina, and Karlo says Elizabeta will come and Elizabeta will be with me, that he's going to work and Elizabeta will come. She'll come on the bus, he says, and then he goes through the door, across the yard and he's gone. And I'm alone. I look at the window, through the window, at the yard. And I'm alone. Then I look at the door that is open. I see the hall, the mirror on the nail. Then I look at the Telefunken that is black. Karlo says that the Telefunken is black when it's switched off, that the lights on the gondola are black when they're switched off. And the closet. I see the closet. And the door to the pantry. That's where the drops are, that's where the milk is and Karlo's accordion, that's where *Nono* used to be, whom I didn't know, who has never been in our kitchen. He was in the pantry, Mama says, when they used to shut him in there when he broke things because he was drunk.

Then Elizabeta comes. Always when Karlo goes to work, Elizabeta comes. And she's with me and she talks to me. She says she'll tell me a nice story, and she talks. She says that her mama was called Marija and that she was also the mother of my mama, Ivanka, who is already in heaven. Elizabeta says that her mama, Marija, was my *nona*, that she lived in Ajdovščina, but not in the town, slightly higher up, below Mount Čaven. Elizabeta says that my *nona*, Marija, had a husband who was my *nono* and that he was called Stanko and he was Elizabeta's *tata*. Elizabeta says that *Nona* Marija was very happy when Elizabeta and my mama went to Trieste and got a job there. Elizabeta says that *Nona* Marija was a farmer and that *Nono* Stanko was also a farmer and that they had a field, vineyards and an orchard and a stable with a cow, which was not called Greta. Then Elizabeta says that *Nona* Marija had a closet in the room and she always wrote inside the door whenever something important happened. She wrote with a pencil, says Elizabeta, if it was important. When the cow had a calf, or there was a drought, or if there was a lot of snow. She wrote everything down with a pencil, says Elizabeta. In the closet, on the door, the inside of it, so that it couldn't be seen from the outside when the door was closed. And then at Shrovetide, Elizabeta says, when people in fancy dress walked by, she said: Oooh, how beautiful they are, and she sat down and she died. And then Elizabeta says that she and my mama, who is already in heaven, let her rest in peace, says Elizabeta, her and my mama used to go from Trieste to Ajdovščina on foot to visit *Nona* Marija. And that they brought her some fruit if there had been hail that destroyed the fruit trees, and *Nona* Marija had written in the closet that there had been hail, which ruined all the fruit and vines, and that *Nono* got drunk out of sadness.

I look at her, Aunt Elizabeta, who is like my mama. She's sitting by the stove. I see her. She talks to me with her hands on her knees. Then when Karlo comes she goes. Karlo comes and she goes. And it's evening, says Karlo, as he turns on the Telefunken and watches the weather on Ljubljana and says it will rain, but not yet, tomorrow. Then he watches the Telefunken and says that I won't be at home for long, that Elizabeta is also old and that he's at work and can't look after me. Then he stops talking and first looks at the Telefunken and then tells me that I should watch it as well. And I watch, and then I don't watch any more and I'm standing in the corner and wait to stand in front of the window in the room, looking at the yard. I think the birds are already sleeping. Then Karlo is talking again and says that Josipina can't look after me either, that she has a husband, that Giacomino is a little crazy and may hit her if she leaves home.

Then he says we're all a little crazy. That I'm a little crazy, but he loves me, so he must be a little crazy, too, instead of putting me in the hospital so that others can look after me. Then he turns off the Telefunken and says that it's all stupid and that we're going to bed.

We walk upstairs, first we're in the hall, then on the stairs and then in the room and then Karlo takes my clothes off and says he'll give me my nightie. I know, that's what he'll do and he'll tell me not to wet myself, that Elizabeta can't wash me every day, that soap costs money and that it isn't healthy to wash so often. Then he leaves me there, in front of the window and I look at the yard and the tree top and the field and the cherry tree, and then I think that Karlo will be by the field where potatoes grow, and he'll talk to Uncle Feliks, to Aunt Lucija, to Franc who is my *tata*, and to my mama. If the moon comes out. Then I think that I mustn't wake him if I see him. And then I lie down and no one says, Good night, Ballerina, sweet dreams. And I know I won't dream and if I don't dream, I won't sleep and if I don't sleep, then I'll throw things at the kitchen door and Karlo said that I'm crazy, that he loves me, but things can't go on like this and I'll go to the hospital.

And then it's a new day and I know I've wet myself, and Elizabeta washes me and changes me and then says she won't come any more and I think she's going to heaven, too, and I want to stand on tiptoe. I go to the corner, step on tiptoe and I look at the yard and I want to sing, together with Mama, who is just like Elizabeta, but Elizabeta doesn't sing and then my toes hurt and I grab what I can and hurl it at the door so that it breaks and then one new day, Elizabeta doesn't come.

I'm sitting in the kitchen eating biscuits brought by Josipina, and I can't see Elizabeta. Karlo is there in the yard, bending over, picking something up. I see. He's carrying something, he comes through the kitchen door. He says it's a bird, that it's a migratory bird and that it's tired, that it can't fly, that it fell into the yard and that it's big, he says. He's holding it in his hands, looking at it. I think it has fallen from the tree top, where it went to sleep, the bird, and that it dreamed and fell and Karlo picked it up. I look at him. He's holding it and looking at it. Then he moves and says we'll put it on the bed where Mama used to sleep for a rest, that its wing is broken or it's just tired. Then he looks at it and goes through the door. I see him. He walks up the stairs in his pants dirty from tree sap, holding a big bird that fell into the yard and shouting for me to wait, to stay in the kitchen, not to be afraid, that he will be back very soon. And then he comes and looks at me. And we look at each other. I'd like to push him into the hall, I'd pinch him, I'd pull his ear. And then I just look at him and he talks. He says he's off work, he took a vacation and thank God that he's on vacation because he knows what to do with birds if they're tired, that he knows all the animals, that he once treated another Greta, which was a cow and was also big.

Now it's evening. I'm dressed in my nightie and wearing my slippers with a butterfly. Karlo is upstairs in his hole. Asleep. I know. I'm standing in front of the door that is ajar. I see the bed. There's no Mama and no Franc. There's the bird that is tired, I know. Karlo said he would put it on the bed where Mama used to sleep. I lift my hand, I see I'm lifting my hand and opening the door and I see it, the bird, on the bed. It isn't sleeping. It looks at me. Its eyes are shining in the dark because there is the moon outside and the eyes of the birds in the tree top are also shiny, but they don't fall into the yard because they're not tired, and when it's a new day they fly off, and I see them, I watch them through the window in the kitchen and I see them fly off, grazing in the field, on the cherry tree and then they come back when it's evening and when I'm in my room and I look through the window and Mama is not here, because she's in heaven. The bird is lying there, looking at me. It has a long neck, the bird on the bed, and a long beak. Karlo says it's not a woodpecker. I know it's not a woodpecker because there's a woodpecker in Elizabeta's garden, where there are also squirrels and benches on which Mrs. Sprigge used to sit. Karlo says it's a bird that lives by the water and that it looks like a stork, which brings babies into the cabbage when cabbage is growing in the field and Karlo has already picked the potatoes and the beans. I look at the bird on the bed. It's lying across the whole bed and I walk over. It's looking at me and its eye is shiny and it isn't moving and I think it's calm.

And then Karlo comes, I hear him. I hear footsteps. He's behind me. Talking. He's talking quietly like he talks to Feliks who comes from heaven and is in the field among the beans and Karlo talks quietly to him so that I can't understand. Quietly he tells me to let it rest, to go to bed, that we will wait a few more days to see if it recovers, that otherwise we would have to take it to the institute so that they can have a good look at it, that he's on vacation and can look after it. Then I go and I'm in my room, lying on the bed and staring at the ceiling that is light from the moon and I know that in the other room there is a bird lying on my mama's bed and I think it's singing and I hear it, and then I go to sleep.

Karlo is in the kitchen. He's doing something with his hand, shaking something into a dish and stirring, and he says that the bird will now eat. Then he says that his vacation is finished, that I'll have to go to hospital. I don't know what vacation is, I don't know what hospital is unless they come to the kitchen and say: Come with us, Ballerina. And they take me out of the kitchen, across the yard, along the road to the town where the sea is, says Karlo. Then he goes upstairs and says he'll be back soon. And he's back soon and says the bird is well, it's standing on Mama's bed and looking through the window. Then he says he'll bring it to the kitchen in the evening, that it'll eat with us, that he's made some pasta and if pasta is good enough for us, it's good enough for the bird.

And now it's evening, I know. The light is on in the kitchen. And we're eating pasta. I see Karlo at the table and the bird by the door. Karlo says it's eating, it's healthy. I see the bird eating by the door. And then Karlo turns on the Telefunken and watches the weather on Ljubljana. He always says: We'll watch Ljubljana, it's a good picture and they don't talk nonsense. And then we watch the Telefunken and the bird jumps onto a chair. Suddenly it opens its wings, which are wide, and it jumps onto the chair and also watches the Telefunken. The weather on Ljubljana. Karlo laughs. I see him, Karlo, who is my brother, laughing and I'm calm. Then he says:

Good job no one can see us. They'd say we're a little silly if they saw a bird by the table, watching the Telefunken. They'd say we're not quite right. *Mamma mia*, Ballerina, it's good we're alone.

Now it's night. I'm lying in bed. Karlo said that the bird stayed in the kitchen, that he'd left the door open, in case it wants to walk around a little, he said. I'm not asleep. I know the bird isn't in the room where Mama used to sleep any more. I know that the bird is in the kitchen and that Karlo is in his hole. Then I hear it, suddenly. I hear it tottering. I hear it. It's in the kitchen, tottering. Still. Now it must be in the hall. I think it's above the sink, looking at itself in the mirror that hangs on a nail. Then I hear frrrrr, the birds sleeping in the tree also do this. Frrrr, when they fly off. Then I hear it totter again. It's on the doorstep. It's tottering on wet ground. Because it has rained, says Karlo. Karlo says that on Ljubljana they always get the weather right. If they say it'll rain, there is rain and it falls and then everything is wet.

I hear it. Slosh—slosh on the wet ground. Then I hear Karlo, too. I hear his footsteps. They're getting closer. He's here. I see him in the door. Ballerina, are you asleep? he asks, and then sees my eyes are open and he says:

Come, you'll see it go. It'll fly away.

I get up and think of Ivan, who will cure me, and I walk toward the window. Karlo is already there. The window is light. Karlo says he put on the light in the yard so that we can see the bird fly off. The window is getting nearer. It's light in the window, I see.

Karlo and I are standing by the window, looking at the yard.

Look, he says and leans closer to the glass. I see it. It's standing in the yard and looking around, the bird with the long neck. And I think it's Mama looking after Albert, who left on a plane to Australia. I think I can see her, who has a thin, thin neck, and she flies away.

14

I'M WALKING in the hail. *Nona* Marija is writing on the closet door that the hail has destroyed everything and that it looked like snow in the morning. Bits of ice are rolling next to my feet. I see my feet, I watch them, I see slippers with a butterfly moving among the hail stones. I see the sky that is black and I know Mama put an under-shirt on me and said it's cold and I have to wear an undershirt so that I don't catch a cold. I'm walking around the orchard in the hail. *Nona* Marija says that the hail has knocked all the apples off the trees and now they're lying in the grass. I'm walking in the hail, looking at the ground. I see the hail, I see the apples in the grass. I bend over. I see my hand grab an apple. I look at it. It's in front of my eyes. I bite into it. The apple is sweet. I go on biting and looking at the hail in the grass. Then it's evening and I see the moon on the black sky and the orchard, the grass and the hail, and suddenly I see a face. I don't know him, he has never been in our kitchen. He's coming closer. His eyes and his mouth are coming closer. I see them in front of me, so close, so very close. And then his mouth attaches itself to my face. I feel it on my forehead, on my eyes, on my neck, on my mouth. At first his mouth is slightly open, I feel his teeth, then the mouth opens like mine and I feel that apple pips are rolling around our mouths. I know I had them in my mouth after the apple was gone because it was sweet. Now the pips are rolling into his mouth. I feel them escaping, and I see the sky and the moon in it and I know that the fruit in the orchard has been destroyed by the hail, and I wake up, suddenly. I'm not scared, I just need to pee.

Then I'm in the kitchen. I'm looking at the yard. Karlo is there, coming into the kitchen. Now he's in the hall, and now in the door. He looks at me. Ballerina, you've got a visitor, he says. He hasn't been here for many years, he says, laughing. You'll be happy, he says, you'll be happy, Ballerina.

And then he walks toward me and we both look at the door. Karlo is behind me, I know. He's holding my shoulders. I'm sitting and he's standing behind me like Mama, who's already in heaven.

And suddenly a man is standing in the door. I don't know him, but I know it's Ivan. He's here. Ivan, who will cure me, has come. And then I'll go to school and I'll be a good girl, like Mama says, and I won't pee in my bed and I won't throw plates at the door and when the postman comes I won't be scared anymore and I won't stand on tiptoe and sing.

Now I'm looking at him, at Ivan, in the door. I'm sitting, looking at him. His head is high, his arms are long, so are his legs and his shoes. Karlo says Ivan is big now, he has a big car and wants to take me on a trip, says Karlo. I see him, Karlo, my brother, who's on vacation, I see him how he laughs now by the window, looking at Ivan in the door. Ivan says we have aged. I hear him. Ready to retire, says Karlo and smiles. Then they talk, Karlo and Ivan. Karlo says that Ballerina is still the same, that he will have to take her to the hospital because there's no one to look after her, that Elizabeta is very old and that Josipina can't do it either. Then he offers Ivan a drink, like to the postman when he comes. Karlo puts the glass on the table and pours the brandy. He says it's home-made. He always says that when it's evening and he's drinking and says it's healthy, helps you digest, and that it's even healthier if it's home-made.

And then I look at Ivan. He tips the glass, smiles, and then says: Shall we go, Ballerina?

And then Karlo dresses me and talks in my ear, quietly like to Uncle Feliks, who is in heaven. Karlo dresses me in the dress with the bow and puts my sneakers on, he says I'll be more comfortable if we go walking. He says I must behave nicely, that I mustn't stand on tiptoe and sing when I'm with Ivan. He says Ivan has become a fine gentleman, that he has a big car and a gold chain around his neck and a gold ring on his finger and that I must be good when I'm with him, because it's very nice that he's taking me on a trip for a whole day.

I don't know what a whole day is, I don't know what a trip is. I'm listening to Karlo. I'm in the room and I'm listening and looking through the window and I see the yard and the chestnut tree and the hills and then the valley that Mama loves so much and says it's nice there, and then Karlo says that there's a car in the yard, that I can see it. Karlo says the car is red and a sports car, that it goes a hundred and forty an hour.

And then I'm in the hall and Ivan is looking at me, saying let's go.

Now I'm sitting in the car with Ivan. I'm strapped in and Ivan tells me that we're going a hundred and forty an hour and that his car is called Lancia. He says we're going along the big road to Sistiana for an ice-cream and then we'll go and see something nice and in the evening we'll go to Trieste and then we'll go to sleep, that it'll be a very nice day. I see the road, I see trees, I see cars flying past me and disappearing. Ivan says I shouldn't be scared, that I'm strapped in and that nothing bad can happen to me. And then he puts on the Grundig and music can be heard. Ivan says that it's good music, it's rock and that everyone listens to it. Then I don't look at the road, I don't look at the escaping trees, I'm looking at Ivan. I see his face. He has long hair, longer than Karlo. Ivan has ears that stick out, he has a chain around his neck and a ring on his finger, a gold one, says Karlo. Ivan is rocking his head and whistling and then he laughs and says the car is a rocket and next year he'll buy a new one, which will go even faster so that he'll be able to get to Venice in an hour.

And then he says:

Are you happy, Ballerina? Do you like it?

And then I think he's going to cure me.

Now we're sitting in a bar. I don't see people. No one is looking at me. Ivan says he's ordered ice-cream, three scoops for each of us, and cream and *amarena*. He says it's nice, sitting in a bar, that he's always sitting in a bar, looking at the *signorinas*, he says that in Trieste there are beautiful *signorinas* and that they don't create too many problems. Ivan says he just whistles and the *signorinas* come and there are no problems.

And then he says I should eat the ice-cream with a spoon and he puts the spoon in my hand. He says ice-cream is eaten with a spoon. And then I eat. I'm pressing the spoon in my fist and grabbing the ice-cream and eating, and I can feel the ice-cream running down my chin and then Ivan says haven't you learnt how to eat yet, aren't you ashamed, you're like a child, he says that he won't take me on a trip

again, if I let ice-cream run down my chin. Then he says he has to
pay. I watch his hands. I look at his ring and I want to stand on tiptoe,
I want to be in the kitchen, in the corner, standing on tiptoe and I
want to sing, I want Mama to sing with me. Then I know I mustn't,
because Karlo said I mustn't.

Now we're in the car, like before. Ivan says that we're driving over
two hundred an hour and then he says that it's a shitty world, where
it's enough to have money and a good car and that it doesn't fucking
matter whether you go to school or not, that it's even worse if you
do go to school, because then you understand even better how the
world is shitty.

I'm looking through the window and I know it's evening. I'm
thinking about the yard and the birds that are going to sleep. I think
of Josipina who will sleep with them in the tree and suddenly I'm
scared that Giacomino will slap her.

Then I'm sitting at a table. Ivan says we're in a restaurant and
we'll eat *gnocchi*. And then he stops talking and looking at me. He's
looking around, but doesn't say anything. I don't see people, they
don't look at me, no one does, not even Ivan. We're alone. I know.
Me and Ivan, who will cure me.

Then he says that the *gnocchi* were good and that we're driving to
Trieste and then he stops talking and doesn't turn on the Grundig.

Then he says that we're going out, that we've arrived and we'll
walk to the sea, that it'll be nice, that everyone will be by the sea, the
whole of Trieste.

And we walk. I see lots of people. Everyone is walking toward the
sea, says Ivan. He says all the streets are full of people and everyone
is walking toward the sea, like us. I look at the street in front of me.
I see people, I see heads and past the heads I see blue and Ivan says
that's the sea, that we're going there.

Now we're by the sea, says Ivan. He says we're in the first row, that
it's much nicer if you're in the first row. I see the sea in front of me,
then I turn around and see people. Ivan says that the crowd is as big
as the sea and then he tells me I will have to look in the air, at the sky,
that I'll see lights and it'll be nice.

I'm standing by the sea, looking in the air, looking at the sky, I know. The sky is there. Mama was always looking in the air when she said that the sky was cloudy or that there's fog over her valley, that there are clouds. Mama was always looking in the air, I know. When she said that *Tata* was in heaven, she was looking in the air, I know.

Everything is quiet now. Ivan, too. He's standing next to me and he's quiet and he's looking in the air, and he says everyone is looking in the air and there will be a bang. Now.

There's a thunder and whistling and suddenly I see lights in the sky. Like on the gondola, only there's a thousand of them here. Ivan says there are more than a thousand, that you can't count them. I watch the lights, there are more than a thousand, and Ivan says that they're in all colors and I think that Mrs. Sprigge will count them. If she counted the stones in the garden at Elizabeta's, she'll count all the lights, there in England. And then Ivan says that they're *fuochi d'artificio*, fireworks in our language. And everyone says Oooh and they clap.

15

KARLO SAYS I'VE been in hospital for a few months now, that they've put me in the cellar because I was screaming and singing and I threw around everything I could find. I see him, Karlo. He's standing by my bed, dressed in blue. I see long lights behind him that are sometimes also blue and sometimes they flicker because there's no contact, Karlo says, and laughs. I'm lying down. I know I'm lying down and Karlo is in front of the bed. He says I'm alone in this room in the cellar and that it's nice if you can be in your own room in a hospital and other people can't bother you. Karlo says I'm a real lady, a real madam, a real *signorina*. If I wasn't a little crazy, I could be home, says Karlo. If I didn't break things and sing so loudly, I could be home, he says. Then he says I'm crazy and I'm here so that they can bring me to my senses, he says. Then he says he's brought me oranges, magazines and Coca Cola. He says that he shouldn't have brought the Coca Cola, because they don't want me to drink it, because it makes me nervous, he says. But I laugh when he tells me he's brought me Coca Cola. I know I'm laughing. Then he says he must go, he doesn't have any free days left, that he must work and that Josipina will come and then on Sunday everyone will come, including Srečko, who has been found after a year. Karlo says that they found him in Bavaria, at a farm near some woods. Then he says he's going to work and Josipina will come later and then Elizabeta will come the next day because someone will bring her with a car. She's old, says Karlo. She has to be brought with a car.

Then I'm alone and I think it's the morning. There's no window, but I think in this room it's always morning, because the light is blue. And it flashes and I think that when it flashes, it'll be day any moment and it'll be night any moment, and then I close my eyes. I know Josipina will come, like every day, because she says Giacomino has nothing against her coming to see me. I know Josipina will come and will put cream on my bottom. Josipina also says that Nivea cream is the best. Even for the sores on my bottom. Josipina says I have sores because I'm lying so much, because I don't get up, because

I don't want to get up and then I moan in pain. Josipina says that I go aaaah, very quietly, I moan aaah, but it can still be heard in the corridor, on the way to the boiler room. She says water gets heated there and then it runs through all the radiators in the hospital. That is why it's sometimes so warm in here, in my room.

I wet myself. And I know that when I've wet myself it's a new day. I don't want to get up and they say I can't get up, either. I don't want to think of Ivan, who will cure me. I want to be like this. I want to lie and sleep and dream that I'm in the kitchen, standing on tiptoe, my toes hurting, and then I sing and throw whatever I can find at the door. Even a knife, which then sticks in the door and Karlo gets angry because he has just sharpened it.

Then I'm in the room, I think, where the window is and below the window there's the chestnut tree, where the birds sleep, and there's the field where Karlo walks and talks to Uncle Feliks and there's the cherry tree, and then there's the meadow and high grasses and crickets. And then there's night and the moon that I can't see, and there's so many bad things in the world because man has landed on the moon with the Sputnik and *Tata* bought a Telefunken and the kitchen was full of people who were watching people come to the moon with the Sputnik. And then they left and I didn't know them because they'd never been in our kitchen before.

And then Josipina comes, like every day, and puts Nivea cream on my bottom, and combs my hair and says she combs my hair so that our Ballerina looks nice. And then I leaf through the magazines. Josipina leafs through them, but she says it's me doing it, that I'm looking at the magazine and reading what's going on in the world, but it's her who's reading and leafing and I wait to see Greta Garbo or Gina Lollobrigida, for Josipina to tell me about the stable with the cow and about *Nona* Marija, who died below Mount Čaven at Shrovetide and who used to write down important things in the closet. Then Josipina says there's nothing to read, there's only bad things, it's better if we don't read, better if we live just as we are, happy. I watch her and listen to her, Josipina, and I think I'm sad and I feel tears on my face. Then I know they're tears because Josipina takes a handkerchief, which is ironed, and she opens it up and wipes my face and says they are tears and they need to be wiped so that they don't slide down onto the floor and break. And then Josipina laughs, after she has put cream on my bottom and combed my hair. She laughs and she tells me she now goes to the theater, secretly, because Giacomino doesn't like it. She tells him she's going to see me, but she goes to the theater, she says. Oh, if only you knew how nice it is, how big and how good the actors are in there. Then she laughs and says that if she was young, she'd become an actress like Greta Garbo or Gina Lollobrigida, whom I never see any more, like Charlie Chaplin and Laurel and Hardy. Then she says she has a boyfriend, who goes to the theater with her because he has a car and can quickly drive her home. He drops her off at the church and she runs home and Giacomino thinks that she came on the bus. And then Josipina looks in the bedside cabinet. And she sees Coca Cola and she laughs and says I shouldn't be drinking Coca Cola, and then she opens it and we both drink Coca Cola and belch, here in the cellar in this light that is blue. Josipina also says the light is blue, and she belches, but quietly, and puts her hand in front of her mouth. And then she goes and smiles. And she says, I'll see you tomorrow. And I'm happy because I drank Coca Cola and belched and I'll wet myself and it'll be a new day and I'll be here, in bed, looking at the light that is blue and I'll think that Mama, who is already in heaven, is coming.

Now it's Sunday. Karlo says everyone has come, and he looks at me. And then I see everyone is standing around the bed and I think it's my party. They're laughing. Elizabeta is here as well. She's looking at me and stroking my face. She's like Mama, who's not here because she's in heaven. And she can't come to the hospital, even though it's Sunday, and Karlo can't bring her with the car either. Because Mama says heaven is high in the air, up among the stars and if it has taken them so long to land on the moon, God only knows how long they would need to get to heaven, says Mama who isn't here.

Then Elizabeta sits down, she sits on a chair, puts her hands on her knees and says: O-la-la. Then Josipina brings me flowers and puts them in a vase on the bedside cabinet and sits on the bed, looking at me. Karlo is standing. Karlo, my brother, who drives Elizabeta with the car, because she's old. I look at them and then I see Srečko, too. He's standing at the end of the room under the blue light that is flickering. Srečko is looking at me, laughing. Srečko doesn't have any hair or teeth anymore, but he's handsome, I know he's handsome because Mama, who isn't here, says so. I see her, we're standing by the window and looking at the hill and the valley that is hers and the mountain that is Angel Mountain, and Mama says that Srečko is handsome in here, and she points at her heart, where it hurts because *Tata* went to heaven and he was covered with a white sheet, at the bar.

And then I see Ivan, too. Ciao, Ballerina, shall we go for a spin? And I smile. I know. I can feel on my face that I am smiling, and I want to be in the kitchen, to see the yard, and I want to stand on tiptoe to see over Mama's shoulder, and I want to sing:

Vooolareee, o, o!

Cantareee, o, o, o, o!

And then everyone sings. Josipina, Karlo, Elizabeta, Srečko, who is also crying, and Ivan, who is laughing and who has a gold chain around his neck.

Vooolaree, o, o!

Cantareee, o, o, o, o!

And then everyone claps, everyone, and Ivan says that I'm a good girl, that I'm not only a ballerina, that I'm also a singer. And then I turn. I know I'm turning. And I see the vase with the flowers that Josipina brought, and I know I'll pick it up, I'll throw it at the door where Ivan is. I know I'll pick it up and I'll throw it at him, at the door, at his head so that it blows up, and then Karlo will say: Don't be stupid, *porca puttana*, you'll kill the man. I know that that is how it'll be. I see him on the floor now, Ivan, who will cure me, I see him holding his head, I see his chain and the ring on his hand and I think I'm having a good time, that I want to drink Coca Cola and that I will belch.

I know it's a new day. Josipina is putting Nivea on my bottom and says that sooner or later we all have to go to heaven and that time goes quickly. I'm lying on my stomach and she's telling me this, while putting Nivea on my sores. She says I haven't got up from the bed for months now, that I don't leaf through magazines and that I don't want to eat and, if things go on as they are, I'll go to heaven, alone. I look at her. I see that she's laughing, that she isn't drinking Coca Cola with me and that she's leaving.

Then I look at the ceiling that is white and blue, and I no longer feel my legs, I no longer feel my arms and I don't know that I'm lying. Karlo is with me now. He's looking at me. Josipina is with him. They say I've died and then they don't say anything else. Josipina is crying and Karlo is looking away, at the door. Then someone else comes, who hasn't been in our kitchen, puts his hand on my eyes and says that they would tie a scarf around my head to close my eyes and that all those who would like to see me for the last time can look at me for an hour, because they will then put me in a coffin. I hear Karlo speak. He says he knows the doctor, that he's a Slovene, that he sings in a choir in Nabrežina.

I'm cold. I think it's winter and I don't have stockings on. I think it's a moonless and starless night, I think I won't be able to see Karlo by the field, talking to Uncle Feliks. I think Mama forgot to put on my stockings.

Then I hear bells. I know I'm being carried to the church. I hear the bells and the organ. Then I hear Karlo say that something will have to be given to the priest and those that will put me in my grave. At least some money to buy a liter of wine, he says. Then I hear Josipina. She says they will have to invite people back to her home, she's made some soup. And then I listen to the priest. Let us pray! he says. And I hear them praying and suddenly I hear a voice I don't know. I know it has been in our kitchen, that voice. I know, I hear it. Then I recognize it. It's far, but I hear it. Srečko, singing. Quietly, but I hear him and I think that he's singing something by Beethoven, because Srečko knows everything by Beethoven.

Then I hear someone say Shush! and Srečko stops singing and I'm sad because it hurts, my heart hurts, where Mama puts her hand when she stands by the window and looks at the yard.

Now they're lowering me down, I can feel it. I feel that I'm falling deep and I think I'm in the earth, because it can be no other way, says

Karlo. First you go into the earth and then, if everything is right, you go to heaven, if you have earned it.

And I hear a voice. It speaks. It says that with Ballerina, one has left us that we didn't know was among us. She left just as unnoticeably as she lived. Then it says that Ballerina, like all her family, was honest, that she was ours and that we didn't really know that she was there. She departed just as unnoticeably as she lived and left a big gap in our community. Then I hear Karlo. Karlo is speaking quietly. What nonsense, what claptrap they're saying, *puttana eva*, says Karlo quietly. Let her rest in peace, says the voice, and then I hear them sing. I don't want them to sing, I don't want to listen to them, I want to be in the kitchen, I want to be in front of the window to be able to see the yard and the tree where the birds sleep, and the field and the hills and the valley, Mama's valley. And then they stop singing, suddenly. Then I hear them throwing soil over me. Mama says I also threw soil on Uncle Feliks, but I was still a little girl and I was still talking and playing and going to school.

Then they aren't singing any more. And I'm happy, because, if everything is right, I'll go to heaven and Mama will sing with me.

And then they're gone, the ones that sang. It's just Karlo. I know he's still here because he's talking. I hear him. He says I should cover myself, because down here where I am, there's a big draft, always. That I may catch a cold, he says, because it's full of holes and that they should be filled in, these holes in the earth, he says. And then he says he's going, going to get the filler to fill this earth in a bit, so that I won't be cold as it's so drafty. And I cover myself up.

MICHAL AJVAZ, *The Golden Age.*
The Other City.

PIERRE ALBERT-BIROT, *Grabinoulor.*

YUZ ALESHKOVSKY, *Kangaroo.*

FELIPE ALFAU, *Chromos.*
Locos.

IVAN ÂNGELO, *The Celebration.*
The Tower of Glass.

ANTÓNIO LOBO ANTUNES,
Knowledge of Hell.
The Splendor of Portugal.

ALAIN MRIAS-MISSON, *Theatre of Incest.*

JOHN ASHBERY AND JAMES SCHUYLER,
A Nest of Ninnies.

ROBERT ASHLEY, *Perfect Lives.*

GABRIELA AVIGUR-ROTEM,
Heatwave and Crazy Birds.

DJUNA BARNES, *Ladies Almanack.*
Ryder.

JOHN BARTH, *Letters.*
Sabbatical.

DONALD BARTHELME, *The King.*
Paradise.

SVETISLAV BASARA, *Chinese Letter.*

MIQUEL BAUÇÀ, *The Siege in the Room.*

RENÉ BELLETTO, *Dying.*

MAREK BIEŃCZYK, *Transparency.*

ANDREI BITOV, *Pushkin House.*

ANDREJ BLATNIK, *You Do Understand.*

LOUIS PAUL BOON, *Chapel Road.*
My Little War.
Summer in Termuren.

ROGER BOYLAN, *Killoyle.*

IGNÁCIO DE LOYOLA Brandão,
Anonymous Celebrity.
Zero.

BONNIE BREMSER, *Troia: Mexican Memoirs.*

CHRISTINE BROOKE-ROSE,
Amalgamemnon.

BRIGID BROPHY, *In Transit.*

GERALD L. BRUNS,
Modern Poetry and the Idea of Language.

GABRIELLE BURTON, *Heartbreak Hotel.*

MICHEL BUTOR, *Degrees,*
Mobile.

G. CABRERA INFANTE,
Infante's Inferno.
Three Trapped Tigers.

JULIETA CAMPMPOS,
The Fear of Losing Eurydice.

ANNE CARSON, *Eros the Bittersweet.*

ORLY CASTEL-BLOOM, *Dolly City.*

LOUIS-FERDINAND CÉLINE,
Castle to Castle.
Conversations with Professor Y,
London Bridge,
Normance,
North,
Rigadoon.

MARIE CHAIX,
The Laurels of Lake Constance.

HUGO CHARTERIS, *The Tide Is Right.*

ERIC CHEVILLARD, *Demolishing Nisard.*

MARC CHOLODENKO, *Mordechai Schamz.*

JOSHUA COHEN, *Witz.*

EMILY HOLMES COLEMAN,
The Shutter of Snow.

ROBERT COOVER, *A Night at the Movies.*

STANLEY CRAWFORD, *Log of the S.S,*
The Mrs Unguentine,
Some Instructions to My Wife.

RENÉ CREVEL, PUTTING *My Foot in It.*

RALPH CUSACK, *Cadenza.*

NICHOLAS DELBANCO,
The Count of Concord,
Sherbrookes.

NIGEL DENNIS, *Cards of Identity.*

PETER DIMOCK,
A Short Rhetoric for Leaving the Family.

ARIEL DORFMFMAN, *Konfidenz.*

COLEMAN DOWELL, *Island People,*
Too Much Flesh and Jabez.

ARKADII DRAGOMOSHCHENKO,
Dust.

RIKKI DUCORNET,
The Complete Butcher's Tales,
The Fountains of Neptune,
The Jade Cabinet,
Phosphor in Dreamland.

WILLIAM EASTLAKE, *The Bamboo Bed,*
Castle Keep,
Lyric of the Circle Heart.

JEAN ECHENOZ, *Chopin's Move.*

STANLEY ELKIN, *A Bad Man,*
Criers and Kibitzers, Kibitzers and Criers,
The Dick Gibson Show,
The Franchiser,
The Living End,
Mrs. Ted Bliss.

FRANÇOIS EMMMMANUEL,
Invitation to a Voyage.

SALVADOR ESPRIU,
Ariadne in the Grotesque Labyrinth.

LESLIE A. FIEDLER,
Love and Death in the American Novel.

JUAN FILLOY, *Op Oloop.*

ANDY FITCH, *Pop Poetics.*

GUSTAVE FLAUBERT,
Bouvard and Pécuchet.

KASS FLEISHER, *Talking out of School.*

FORD MADOX FORD,
The March of Literature.

JON FOSSE, *Aliss at the Fire,*
Melancholy.

MAX FRISCH, *I'm Not Stiller,*
Man in the Holocene.

CARLOS FUENTES, *Christopher Unborn,*
Distant Relations,
Terra Nostra,
Where the Air Is Clear.

TAKEHIKO FUKUNAGA,
Flowers of Grass.

WILLIAM GADDIS, J R, *The Recognitions.*

JANICE GALLOWAY, *Foreign Parts,*
The Trick Is to Keep Breathing.

WILLIAM H H. GASS,
Cartesian Sonata and Other Novellas,
Finding a Form,
A Temple of Texts,
The Tunnel,
Willie Masters' Lonesome Wife.

GÉRARD GAVARRY, *Hoppla! 1 2 3.*

ETIENNE GILSON,
The Arts of the Beautiful, Forms
and Substances in the Arts.

C. S S. GISCOMBE, *Giscome Road,*
Here.

DOUGLAS GLOVER,
Bad News of the Heart.

WITOLD GOMBROWICZ,
A Kind of Testament.

PAULO EMÍLIO SALES GOMES,
P's Three Women.

GEORGI GOSPODINOV, *Natural Novel.*

JUAN GOYTISOLO, *Count Julian,*
Juan the Landless,
Makbara,
Marks of Identity.

HENRY GREEN, *Back,*
Blindness,
Concluding,
Doting,
Nothing.

JACK GREEN, *Fire the Bastards!*

JIŘÍ GRUŠA, *The Questionnaire.*

MELA HARTWIG,
Am I a Redundant Human Being?

JOHN HAWKES, *The Passion Artist,*
Whistlejacket.

ELIZABETH HEIGHWAY, ED.,
Contemporary Georgian Fiction.

ALEKSANDAR HEMON, ED.,
Best European Fiction.

AIDAN HIGGINS, *Balcony of Europe,*
Blind Man's Bluff,
Bornholm Night-Ferry,
Flotsam and Jetsam,
Langrishe, Go Down,
Scenes from a Receding Past.

KEIZO HINO, *Isle of Dreams.*

KAZUSHI HOSAKA, *Plainsong.*

ALDOUS HUXLEY, *Antic Hay,*
Crome Yellow,
Point Counter Point,
Those Barren Leaves,
Time Must Have a Stop.

NAOYUKI II, *The Shadow of a Blue Cat.*

GERT JONKE, *The Distant Sound,*
Geometric Regional Novel,
Homage to Czerny,
The System of Vienna.

JACQUES JOUET, *Mountain R,*
Savage,
Upstaged.

MIEKO KANAI, *The Word Book.*

YORAM KANIUK, *Life on Sandpaper.*

HUGH KENNER, Flaubert,
Joyce and Beckett: The Stoic Comedians,
Joyce's Voices.

DANILO KIS̆, *The Attic,*
Garden, Ashes,
The Lute and the Scars,
Psalm 44,
A Tomb for Boris Davidovich.

ANITA KONKKA, *A Fool's Paradise.*

GEORGE KONRÁD, *The City Builder.*

TADEUSZ KONWICKI,
A Minor Apocalypse,
The Polish Complex.

MENIS KOUMANDAREAS, *Koula.*

ELAINE KRAF, *The Princess of 72nd Street.*

JIM KRUSOE, *Iceland.*

AYŞE KULIN,
Farewell: A Mansion in Occupied Istanbul.

EMILIO LASCANO TEGUI,
On Elegance While Sleeping.

ERIC LAURRENT, *Do Not Touch.*

VIOLETTE LEDUC, *La Bâtarde.*

EDOUARD LEVÉ, *Autoportrait,*
Suicide.

MARIO LEVI, *Istanbul Was a Fairy Tale.*

DEBORAH LEVY, *Billy and Girl.*

JOSE´ LEZAMA LIMA, *Paradiso.*

ROSA LIKSOM, *Dark Paradise.*

OSMAN LINS,
Avalovara,
The Queen of the Prisons of Greece.

ALF MAC LOCHLAINN,
The Corpus in the Library,
Out of Focus.

RON LOEWINSOHN, *Magnetic Field(s).*

MINA LOY, *Stories and Essays of Mina Loy.*

D. KEITH MANO, *Take Five.*

MICHELINE AHARONIAN MARCOM,
The Mirror in the Well.

BEN MARCUS, *The Age of Wire and String.*

WALLACE MARKFIELD, *Teitlebaum's*
Window,
To an Early Grave.

DAVID MARKSON, *Reader's Block,*
Wittgenstein's Mistress.

CAROLE MASO, *AVA.*

LADISLAV MATEJKA &
KRYSTYNA POMORSKA, EDS.,
Readings in Russian Poetics: Formalist and
Structuralist Views.

HARRY MATHEWS, *Cigarettes,*
The Conversions,
The Human Country: New and Collected Stories,
The Journalist,
My Life in CIA,
Singular Pleasures,
The Sinking of the Odradek
Stadium,
Tlooth.

JOSEPH MCELROY,
Night Soul and Other Stories.

ABDELWAHAB MEDDEB, *Talismano.*

GERHARD MEIER, *Isle of the Dead.*

HERMAN MELVILLE, *The Confidence-Man.*

AMANDA MICHALOPOULOU, *I'd Like.*

STEVEN MILLHAUSER,
The Barnum Museum,
In the Penny Arcade.

RALPH J. MILLS, JR., *Essays on Poetry.*

MOMUS, *The Book of Jokes.*

CHRISTINE MONTALBETTI,
The Origin of Man,
Western.

OLIVE MOORE, *Spleen.*

NICHOLAS MOSLEY, *Accident,*
Assassins,
Catastrophe Practice,
Experience and Religion,
A Garden of Trees,
Hopeful Monsters,
Imago Bird,
Impossible Object,
Inventing God,
Judith,
Look at the Dark,
Natalie Natalia,
Serpent,
Time at War.

WARREN MOTTE, *Fables of the Novel: French*
Fiction since 1990,
Fiction Now: The French Novel in the 21st
Century,
Oulipo: A Primer of Potential Literature.

GERALD MURNANE, *Barley Patch,*
Inland.

YVES NAVARRE,
Our Share of Time,
Sweet Tooth.

DOROTHY NELSON, *In Night's City,*
Tar and Feathers.

ESHKOL NEVO, *Homesick.*

WILFRIDO D D. NOLLEDO,
But for the Lovers.

FLANN O'BRIEN, *At Swim-Two-Birds,*
The Best of Myles,
The Dalkey Archive,
The Hard Life,
The Poor Mouth,
The Third Policeman.

CLAUDE OLLIER, *The Mise-en-Scène,*
Wert and the Life Without End.

GIOVANNI ORELLI, *Walaschek's Dream.*

PATRIK OUŘEDNÍK, *Europeana,*
The Opportune Moment, 1855.

BORIS PAHOR, *Necropolis.*

FERNANDO DEL PASO,
News from the Empire,
Palinuro of Mexico.

ROBERT PINGET, *The Inquisitory,*
Mahu or The Material,
Trio.

MANUEL PUIG, *Betrayed by Rita Hayworth,*
The Buenos Aires Affair,
Heartbreak Tango.

RAYMYMOND QUENEAU, *The Last Days,*
Odile,
Pierrot Mon Ami,
Saint Glinglin.

ANN QUIN, *Berg,*
Passages,
Three,
Tripticks.

ISHMAEL REED, *The Free-Lance Pallbearers,*
The Last Days of Louisiana Red,
Ishmael Reed: The Plays,
Juice!,
Reckless Eyeballing,
The Terrible Threes,
The Terrible Twos,
Yellow Back Radio Broke-Down.

JASIA REICHARDT,
15 Journeys Warsaw to London.

NOËLLE REVAZ,
With the Animals.

JOÃO UBALDO RIBEIRO,
House of the Fortunate Buddhas.

JEAN RICARDOU, *Place Names*.

RAINER MARIA RILKE,
  The Notebooks of Malte Laurids Brigge.

JULIÁN RÍOS, *The House of Ulysses*,
  Larva: A Midsummer Night's Babel,
  Poundemonium,
  Procession of Shadows.

AUGUSTO ROA BASTOS, *I the Supreme*.

DANIËL ROBBERECHTS,
  Arriving in Avignon.

JEAN ROLIN,
  The Explosion of the Radiator Hose.

OLIVIER ROLIN, *Hotel Crystal*.

ALIX CLEO ROUBAUD, *Alix's Journal*.

JACQUES ROUBAUD,
  The Form of a City Changes Faster, Alas,
  Than the Human Heart,
  The Great Fire of London,
  Hortense in Exile,
  Hortense Is Abducted,
  The Loop,
  Mathematics, The Plurality of Worlds of Lewis,
  The Princess Hoppy,
  Some Thing Black.

RAYMYMOND ROUSSEL,
  Impressions of Africa.

VEDRANA RUDAN, *Night*.

STIG SÆTERBAKKEN, *Siamese, Self Control*.

LYDIE SALVAYRE, *The Company of Ghosts*,
  The Lecture,
  The Power of Flies.

LUIS RAFAEL SÁNCHEZ,
  Macho Camacho's Beat.

SEVERO SARDUY, *Cobra & Maitreya*.

NATHALIE SARRAUTE,
  Do You Hear Them?,
  Martereau,
  The Planetarium.

ARNO SCHMIDT, *Collected Novellas*,
  Collected Stories,
  Nobodaddy's Children,
  Two Novels.

ASAF SCHURR, *Motti*.

GAIL SCOTT, *My Paris*.

DAMION SEARLS, *What We Were Doing and*
  Where We Were Going.

JUNE AKERS SEESE,
  Is This What Other Women Feel Too?,
  What Waiting Really Means.

BERNARD SHARE, *Inish, Transit*.

VIKTOR SHKLOVSKY, *Bowstring*,
  Knight's Move,
  A Sentimental Journey: Memoirs 1917–1922,
  Energy of Delusion: A Book on Plot,
  Literature and Cinematography,
  Theory of Prose,
  Third Factory,
  Zoo, or Letters Not about Love.

PIERRE SINIAC, *The Collaborators*.

KJERSTI A. SKOMSVOLD,
  The Faster I Walk, the Smaller I Am.

JOSEF S̆KVORECKY̒,
  The Engineer of Human Souls.

GILBERT SORRENTINO,
  Aberration of Starlight,
  Blue Pastoral,
  Crystal Vision,
  Imaginative Qualities of Actual Things,
  Mulligan Stew,
  Pack of Lies,
  Red the Fiend,
  The Sky Changes,
  Something Said,
  Splendide-Hôtel,
  Steelwork,
  Under the Shadow.

W. M. SPACKMAN, *The Complete Fiction*.

ANDRZEJ STASIUK, *Dukla*,
  Fado.

GERTRUDE STEIN, *The Making of Americans*,
  A Novel of Thank You.

LARS SVENDSEN, *A Philosophy of Evil*.

PIOTR SZEWC, *Annihilation*.

GONÇALO M. TAVARES, *Jerusalem*,
  Joseph Walser's Machine,
  Learning to Pray in the Age of Technique.

FOR A FULL LIST OF PUBLICATIONS, VISIT: www.dalkeyarchive.com

LUCIAN DAN TEODOROVICI,
Our Circus Presents . . .

NIKANOR TERATOLOGEN,
Assisted Living.

STEFAN THEMERSON,
Hobson's Island,
The Mystery of the Sardine,
Tom Harris.

TAEKO TOMIOKA, *Building Waves.*

JOHN TOOMEY, *Sleepwalker.*

JEAN-PHILIPPPPE TOUSSAINT,
The Bathroom,
Camera,
Monsieur,
Reticence,
Running Away,
Self-Portrait Abroad,
Television,
The Truth about Marie.

DUMITRU TSEPENEAG,
Hotel Europa,
The Necessary Marriage,
Pigeon Post,
Vain Art of the Fugue.

ESTHER TUSQUETS,
Stranded.

DUBRAVKA UGRESIC,
Lend Me Your Character,
Thank You for Not Reading.

TOR ULVEN, *Replacement.*

MATI UNT,
Brecht at Night,
Diary of a Blood Donor,
Things in the Night.

ÁLVARO URIBE AND OLIVIA SEARS, EDS.,
Best of Contemporary Mexican Fiction.

ELOY URROZ, *Friction,*
The Obstacles.

LUISA VALENZUELA,
Dark Desires and the Others,
He Who Searches.

PAUL VERHAEGHEN,
Omega Minor.

AGLAJA VETERANYI,
Why the Child Is Cooking in the Polenta.

BORIS VIAN, *Heartsnatcher.*

LLORENÇ VILLALONGA, *The Dolls' Room.*

TOOMAS VINT, *An Unending Landscape.*

ORNELA VORPSI,
The Country Where No One Ever Dies.

AUSTRYN WAINHOUSE,
Hedyphagetica.

CURTIS WHITE,
America's Magic Mountain,
The Idea of Home,
Memories of My Father Watching TV,
Requiem.

DIANE WILLIAMS,
Excitability: Selected Stories, Romancer Erector.

DOUGLAS WOOLF,
Wall to Wall,
Ya! & John-Juan.

JAY WRIGHT,
Polynomials and Pollen,
The Presentable Art of Reading Absence.

PHILIP WYLIE, *Generation of Vipers.*

MARGUERITE YOUNG,
Angel in the Forest,
Miss MacIntosh, My Darling.

REYOUNG, *Unbabbling.*

VLADO Z̆ABOT, *The Succubus.*

ZORAN Z̆IVKOVIC´, *Hidden Camera.*

LOUIS ZUKOFSKY, *Collected Fiction.*

VITOMIL ZUPAN, *Minuet for Guitar.*

SCOTT ZWIREN, *God Head.*